COLONEL OF CARTERSVILLE
BY F HOPKINSON SMITH
WITH ILLUSTRATIONS
BY E W KEMBLE AND
THE AUTHOR

BOSTON AND NEW YORK
HOUGHTON, MIFFLIN AND COMPANY
The Riverside Press, Cambridge
1896

FIFTEENTH THOUSAND.

The Riverside Press, Cambridge, Mass., U. S. A.
Electrotyped and Printed by H. O. Houghton & Co.

" My fire is my friend." — *Page 27*.

I dedicate this book to the memory of my counselor and my friend, — that most delightful of story-tellers, that most charming of comrades, — my dear old Mother; whose early life was spent near the shade of the Colonel's porch, and whose keen enjoyment of the stories between these covers — stories we have so often laughed over together — is still among my pleasantest recollections.

F. H. S.

New York, May, 1891.

Contents and List of Illustrations

COLONEL CARTER OF CAR-TERSVILLE

CHAPTER I

The Colonel's House in Bedford Place

THE dinner was at the colonel's — an
old-fashioned, partly furnished, two-story
house nearly a century old which crouches
down behind a larger and more modern
dwelling fronting on Bedford Place within
a stone's throw of the tall clock tower of
Jefferson Market.

The street entrance to this curious abode
is marked by a swinging wooden gate
opening into a narrow tunnel which dodges
under the front house. It is an uncanny
sort of passageway, mouldy and wet from a
long-neglected leak overhead, and is lighted
at night by a rusty lantern with dingy glass
sides.

On sunny days this gruesome tunnel
frames from the street a delightful picture

of a bit of the yard beyond, with the quaint colonial door and its three steps let down in a welcoming way.

Its retired location and shabby entrance brought it quite within the colonel's income, and as the rent was not payable in advance, and the landlord patient, he had surrounded himself not only with all the comforts but with many of the luxuries of a more pretentious home.   In this he was assisted by his negro servant Chad, — an abbreviation of Nebuchadnezzar, — who was chambermaid, cook, butler, body-servant, and boots, and who by his marvelous tales of the magnificence of " de old fambly place in Caartersville" had established a credit among the shopkeepers on the avenue which would have been denied a much more solvent customer.

To this hospitable retreat I wended my way in obedience to one of the colonel's characteristic notes : —

No. 51 BEDFORD PLACE.
Friday.

Everything is booming — Fitz says the scheme will take like the measles — dinner tomorrow at six — don't be late.

CARTER.

The colonel had written several similar

notes that week, — I lived but a few streets away, — all on the spur of the moment, and all expressive of his varying moods and wants; the former suggested by his un-bounded enthusiasm over his new railroad scheme, and the latter by such requests as these: "Will you lend me half a dozen napkins — mine are all in the wash, and I want enough to carry me over Sunday. Chad will bring, with your permission, the extra pair of andirons you spoke of." Or, "Kindly hand Chad the two magazines and a corkscrew."

Of course Chad always tucked them

under his arm, and carried them away, for nobody ever refused the colonel anything — nobody who loved him. As for himself, he would have been equally generous in return, and have emptied his house, and even his pocketbook, in my behalf, had that latter receptacle been capable of further effort. Should this have been temporarily overstrained, — and it generally was, — he would have promptly borrowed the amount of the nearest friend, and then have rubbed his hands and glowed all day with delight at being able to relieve my necessity.

"I am a Virginian, suh. Command me," was his way of putting it.

So to-night I pushed open the swinging door, felt my way along the dark passage, and crossed the small yard choked with snow at the precise minute when the two hands of the great clock in the tall tower pointed to six.

The door was opened by Chad.

"Walk right in, suh ; de colonel's in de dinin'-room."

Chad was wrong. The colonel was at that moment finishing his toilet upstairs, in what he was pleased to call his "dressing-room," his cheery voice announcing that fact over the balusters as soon as he heard my own, coupled with the additional information that he would be down in five minutes.

What a cosy charming interior, this dining-room of the colonel's! It had once been two rooms, and two very small ones at that, divided by folding doors. From out the rear one there had opened a smaller room answering to the space occupied by the narrow hall and staircase in front. All the interior partitions and doors dividing these three rooms had been knocked away at some time in its history, leaving an L interior having two windows in front and three in the rear.

Some one of its former occupants, more luxurious than the others, had paneled the walls of this now irregular-shaped apartment with a dark wood running half way to the low ceiling badly smoked and blackened by time, and had built two fireplaces — an open wood fire which laughed at me from behind my own andirons, and an old-fashioned English grate set into the chimney with wide hobs — convenient and necessary for the various brews and mixtures for which the colonel was famous.

Midway, equally warmed by both fires, stood the table, its centre freshened by a great dish of celery white and crisp, with covers for three on a snow-white cloth re splendent in old India blue, while at each end shone a pair of silver coasters, — heirlooms from Carter Hall, — one holding a cut-glass decanter of Madeira, the other awaiting its customary bottle of claret.

On the hearth before the wood fire rested a pile of plates, also India blue, and on the mantel over the grate stood a row of bottles adapting themselves, like all good foreigners, to the rigors of our climate. Add a pair of silver candelabra with candles, — the colonel despised gas, — dark red curtains drawn close, three or four easy chairs, a few etchings and sketches loaned from my studio, together with a modest sideboard at the end of the L, and you have the salient features of a room so inviting and restful that you wanted life made up of one long dinner, continually served within its hospitable walls.

But I hear the colonel calling down the back stairs : —

"Not a minute over eighteen, Chad. You ruined those ducks last Sunday."

The next moment he had me by both hands.

"My dear Major, I am pa'alized to think I kep' you waitin'. Just up from my office. Been workin' like a slave, suh. Only five minutes to dress befo' dinner. Have a drop of sherry and a dash of bitters, or shall we wait for Fitzpatrick? No? All right! He should have been here befo' this. You don't know Fitz? Most extraord'nary man; a great mind, suh; literature, science, politics, finance, everything at his fingers' ends. He has been of the greatest service to me since I have been in New York in this railroad enterprise, which I am happy to say is now reachin' a culmination. You shall hear all about it after dinner. Put yo' body in that chair and yo' feet on the fender — my fire and yo' fender! No, Fitz's fender and yo' andirons! Charmin' combination!"

It is always one of my delights to watch the colonel as he busies himself about the room, warming a big chair for his guests, punching the fire, brushing the sparks from the pile of plates, and testing the temperature of the claret lovingly with the palms of his hands.

He is perhaps fifty years of age, tall and slightly built. His iron gray hair is brushed straight back from his forehead, overlapping his collar behind. His eyes are deep-set and twinkling ; nose prominent ; cheeks slightly sunken ; brow wide and high ; and chin and jaw strong and marked. His moustache droops over a firm, well-cut mouth and unites at its ends with a gray goatee which rests on his shirt front.

Like most Southerners living away from great cities his voice is soft and low, and tempered with a cadence that is delicious.

He wears a black broadcloth coat, — a double-breasted garment, — with similar colored waistcoat and trousers, a turn-down collar, a shirt of many plaits which is under-starched and over-wrinkled but always clean, large cuffs very much frayed, a narrow black or white tie, and low shoes with white cotton stockings.

This black broadcloth coat, by the way, is quite the most interesting feature of the colonel's costume. So many changes are constantly made in its general make-up that you never quite believe it is the same ill-buttoned, shiny garment until you become familiar with its possibilities.

When the colonel has a funeral or other serious matter on his mind, this coat is buttoned close up under his chin showing only the upper edge of his white collar, his gaunt throat and the stray end of a black cravat. When he is invited to dinner he buttons it lower down, revealing as well a bit of his plaited shirt, and when it is a wedding this old stand-by is thrown wide open discovering a stiff, starched, white waistcoat with ivory buttons and snowy neck-cloth.

These several make-ups used once to surprise me, and I often found myself insisting that the looseness and grace with which this garment flapped about the colonel's thin legs was only possible in a brand-new coat having all the spring and lightness of youth in its seams. I was always mistaken. I had only to look at the mismated buttons and the raveled edge of the lining fringing the tails. It was the same coat.

The colonel wore to-night the lower-button style with the white tie. It was indeed the adjustment of this necessary article which had consumed the five minutes passed in his dressing-room, slightly lengthened by the time necessary to trim his cuffs — a little nicety which he rarely overlooked and which it mortified him to forget.

What a frank, generous, tender-hearted fellow he is : happy as a boy ; hospitable to the verge of beggary ; enthusiastic as he is visionary ; simple as he is genuine. A Virginian of good birth, fair education, and limited knowledge of the world and of men, proud of his ancestry, proud of his State, and proud of himself ; believing in states' rights, slavery, and the Confederacy ; and away down in the bottom of his soul still clinging to the belief that the poor white trash of the earth includes about everybody outside of Fairfax County.

With these antecedents it is easy to see that his "reconstruction" is as hopeless as that of the famous Greek frieze, outwardly whole and yet always a patchwork. So he chafes continually under what he believes to be the tyranny and despotism of an undefined autocracy, which, in a general way, he calls "the Government," but which really refers to the distribution of certain local offices in his own immediate vicinity.

When he hands you his card it bears this unabridged inscription : —

Colonel George Fairfax Carter,
of Carter Hall,
Cartersville, Virginia.

He omits "United States of America," simply because it would add nothing to his identity or his dignity.

"There's Fitz," said the colonel as a sharp double knock sounded at the outer gate; and the next instant a stout, thick-set, round-faced man of forty, with merry, bead-like eyes protected by big-bowed spectacles, pushed open the door, and peered in good-humoredly.

The colonel sprang forward and seized him by both shoulders.

"What the devil do you mean, Fitz, by comin' ten minutes late? Don't you know, suh, that the burnin' of a canvasback is a crime?

"Stuck in the snow? Well, I'll forgive you this once, but Chad won't. Give me yo' coat — bless me! it is as wet as a setter dog. Now put yo' belated carcass into this chair which I have been warmin' for you, right next to my dearest old friend,

the Major. Major, Fitz! — Fitz, the
Major! Take hold of each other. Does
my heart good to get you both together.
Have you brought a copy of the prospectus
of our railroad? You know I want the
Major in with us on the groun' flo'. But
after dinner — not a word befo'."

This railroad was the colonel's only hope
for the impoverished acres of Carter Hall,
but lately saved from foreclosure by the
generosity of his aunt, Miss Nancy Carter,
who had redeemed it with almost all her
savings, the house and half of the outlying lands being, thereupon, deeded to her.
The other half reverted to the colonel.

I explained to Fitz immediately after his
hearty greeting that I was a humble land-
scape painter, and not a major at all, having
not the remotest connection with any military organization whatever; but that the
colonel always insisted upon surrounding
himself with a staff, and that my promotion
was in conformity with this habit.

The colonel laughed, seized the poker,
and rapped three times on the floor. A
voice from the kitchen rumbled up: —

" Comin', sah! "

It was Chad " dishin' the dinner " below,

his explanations increasing in distinctness as he pushed the rear door open with his foot, — both hands being occupied with the soup tureen which he bore aloft and placed at the head of the table.

In a moment more he retired to the outer hall and reappeared brilliant in white jacket and apron. Then he ranged himself behind the colonel's chair and with great dignity announced that dinner was served.

"Come, Major! Fitz, sit where you can warm yo' back — you are not thawed out yet. One minute, gentlemen, — an old custom of my ancestors which I never omit."

The blessing was asked with becoming reverence; there was a slight pause, and then the colonel lifted the cover of the tureen and sent a savory cloud of incense to the ceiling.

The soup was a cream of something with baby crabs. There was also a fish, — boiled, — with slices of hard boiled eggs fringing the dish, ovaled by a hedge of parsley and supplemented by a pyramid of potatoes with their jackets ragged as tramps. Then a ham, brown and crisp, and bristling all over with cloves.

Then the ducks!

It was beautiful to see the colonel's face when Chad, with a bow like a folding jack-knife, held this dish before him.

"Lay 'em here, Chad — right under my nose. Now hand me that pile of plates sizzlin' hot, and give that caarvin' knife a turn or two across the hearth. Major, dip a bit of celery in the salt and follow it with a mou'ful of claret. It will prepare yo' palate for the kind of food we raise gentlemen on down my way. See that red blood, suh, followin' the knife!"

"Suit you, marsa?" Chad never forgot his slave days.

"To a turn, Chad, — I would n't take a thousand dollars for you," replied the colonel, relapsing as unconsciously into an old habit.

It was not to be wondered at that the colonel loved a good dinner. To dine well was with him an inherited instinct; one of the necessary preliminaries to all the important duties in life. To share with you his last crust was a part of his religion; to eat alone, a crime.

"There, Major," said the colonel as Chad laid the smoking plate before me, "is the breast of a bird that fo' days ago was divin' for wild celery within fo'ty miles of Caarter Hall. My dear old aunt Nancy sends me a pair every week, bless her sweet soul! Fill yo' glasses and let us drink to her health and happiness." Here the colonel rose from his chair: "Gentlemen, the best thing on this earth — a true Southern lady!

"Now, Chad, the red pepper."

"No jelly, Colonel?" said Fitz, with an eye on the sideboard.

"Jelly? No, suh; not a suspicion of it. A pinch of salt, a dust of cayenne, then shut yo' eyes and mouth, and don't open them 'cept for a drop of good red wine. It is the salt marsh in the early mornin' that you are tastin', suh, —not molasses candy. You Nawtherners don't really treat a canvasback with any degree of respect. You ought never to come into his presence when he lies in state without takin' off yo' hats. That may be one reason why he skips over the Nawthern States when he takes his annual fall outin'." And he laughed heartily.

"But you use it on venison?" argued Fitz.

"Venison is diff'ent, suh. That game lives on moose buds, the soft inner bark of the sugar maple, and the tufts of sweet grass. There is a propriety and justice in his endin' his days smothered in sweets; but the wild duck, suh, is bawn of the salt ice, braves the storm, and lives a life of peyil and hardship. You don't degrade a' oyster, a soft shell crab, or a clam with confectionery; why a canvasback duck?

"Now, Chad, serve coffee."

The colonel pushed back his chair, and opened a drawer in a table on his right, producing three small clay pipes with reed stems and a buckskin bag of tobacco. This he poured out on a plate, breaking the coarser grains with the palms of his hands, and filling the pipes with the greatest care.

Fitz watched him curiously, and when he reached for the third pipe, said : —

" No, Colonel, none for me ; smoke a cigar — got a pocketful."

" Smoke yo' own cigars, will you, and in the presence of a Virginian? I don't believe you have got a drop of Irish blood left in yo' veins, or you would take this pipe."

" Too strong for me," remonstrated Fitz.

" Throw that villainous device away, I say, Fitz, and surprise yo' nostrils with a whiff of this. Virginia tobacco, suh, — raised at Caartersville, — cured by my own servants. No ? Well, you will, Major. Here, try that ; every breath of it is a nosegay," said the colonel, turning to me.

" But, Colonel," continued Fitz, with a sly twinkle in his eye, " your tobacco pays no tax. With a debt like ours it is the duty of every good citizen to pay his share of it. Half the cost of this cigar goes to the Government."

It was a red flag to the colonel, and he laid down his pipe and faced Fitz squarely.

" Tax ! On our own productions, suh ! Raised on our own land ! Are you again forgettin' that you are an Irishman and becomin' one of these money-makin' Yankees? Have n't we suffe'd enough — robbed of our property, our lands confiscated, our slaves torn from us; nothin' left but our honor and the shoes we stand in!"

The colonel on cross-examination could

not locate any particular wholesale robbery, but it did not check the flow of his indignation.

"Take, for instance, the town of Caartersville: look at that peaceful village which for mo' than a hundred years has enjoyed the privileges of free government; and not only Caartersville, but all our section of the State."

" Well, what's the matter with Cartersville ? " asked Fitz, lighting his cigar.

" Mattah, suh !   Just look at the degra-
dation it fell into hardly ten years ago.   A
Yankee jedge jurisdictin' our laws, a Yankee sheriff enfo'cin' 'em, and a Yankee
postmaster distributin' letters and sellin'
postage stamps."

" But they were elected all right, Colonel, and represented the will of the people."

" What people?   Yo' people, not mine.
No, my dear Fitz ; the Administration
succeeding the war treated us shamefully,
and will go down to postehity as infa-
mous."

The colonel here left his chair and began
pacing the floor, his indignation rising at
every step.

" To give you an idea, suh," he continued, " of what we Southern people suffe'd
immediately after the fall of the Confederacy, let me state a case that came under
my own observation.

" Colonel Temple Talcott of F'okeer
County, Virginia, came into Talcottville
one mornin', suh, — a town settled by his
ancestors, — ridin' upon his horse — or

rather a mule belongin' to his overseer. Colonel Talcott, suh, belonged to one of the vehy fust families in Virginia. He was a son of Jedge Thaxton Talcott, and grandson of General Snowden Stafford Talcott of the Revolutionary War. Now, suh, let me tell you right here that the Talcott blood is as blue as the sky, and that every gentleman bearin' the name is known all over the county as a man whose honor is dearer to him than his life, and whose word is as good as his bond. Well, suh, on this mornin' Colonel Talcott left his plantation in charge of his overseer, — he was workin' it on shares, — and rode through his estates to his ancestral town, some five miles distant. It is true, suh, these estates were no longer in his name, but that had no bearin' on the events that followed; he ought to have owned them, and would have done so but for some vehy ungentlemanly fo'closure proceedin's which occurred immediately after the war.

"On arriving at Talcottville the colonel dismounted, handed the reins to his servant, — or perhaps one of the niggers around the do', — and entered the post-office. Now, suh, let me tell you that one

month befo', the Government, contrary to
the express wishes of a great many of our
leadin' citizens, had sent a Yankee postmaster to Talcottville to administer the
postal affairs of that town.   No sooner had
this man taken possession than he began
to be exclusive, suh, and to put on airs.
The vehy fust air he put on was to build a
fence in his office and compel our people
to transact their business through a hole.
This in itself was vehy gallin', suh, for
up to that time the mail had always been
dumped out on the table in the stage office
and every gentleman had he'ped himself.
The next thing was the closin' of his mail
bags at a' hour fixed by himself.   This
became a great inconvenience to our citizens, who were often late in finishin' their
correspondence, and who had always found
our former postmaster willin' either to hold
the bag over until the next day, or to send
it across to Drummondtown by a boy to
catch a later train.

"Well, suh, Colonel Talcott's mission to
the post-office was to mail a letter to his
factor in Richmond, Virginia, on business
of the utmost importance to himself, —
namely, the raisin' of a small loan upon

his share of the crop. Not the crop that was planted, suh, but the crop that he expected to plant.

"Colonel Talcott approached the hole, and with that Chesterfieldian manner which has distinguished the Talcotts for mo' than two centuries asked the postmaster for the loan of a three-cent postage stamp.

"To his astonishment, suh, he was refused.

"Think of a Talcott in his own county town bein' refused a three-cent postage stamp by a low-lived Yankee, who had never known a gentleman in his life! The colonel's first impulse was to haul the scoundrel through the hole and caarve him; but then he remembered that he was a Talcott and could not demean himself, and drawin' himself up again with that manner which was grace itself he requested the loan of a three-cent postage stamp until he should communicate with his factor in Richmond, Virginia; and again he was refused. Well, suh, what was there left for a high-toned Southern gentleman to do? Colonel Talcott drew his revolver and shot that Yankee scoundrel through the heart, and killed him on the spot.

"And now, suh, comes the most remarkable part of this story. If it had not been for Major Tom Yancey, Jedge Kerfoot, and myself there would have been a lawsuit."

Fitz lay back in his chair and roared.

"And they did not hang the colonel?"

"Hang a Talcott! No, suh; we don't hang gentlemen down our way. Jedge Kerfoot vehy properly charged the coroner's jury that it was a matter of self-defense, and Colonel Talcott was not detained mo' than haalf an hour."

The colonel stopped, unlocked a closet in the sideboard, and produced a black bottle labeled in ink, "Old Cherry Bounce, 1848."

"You must excuse me, gentlemen, but the discussion of these topics has quite unnerved me. Allow me to share with you a thimbleful."

Fitz drained his glass, cast his eyes upward, and said solemnly, "To the repose of the postmaster's soul."

CHAPTER II

The Garden Spot of Virginia seeks an Outlet to the Sea

CHAD was just entering the small gate which shut off the underground passage when I arrived opposite the colonel's cozy quarters. I had come to listen to the details of that booming enterprise with the epidemic proclivities, the discussion of which had been cut short by the length of time it had taken to kill the postmaster the night before.

It was quite evident that the colonel expected guests, for Chad was groaning under a square wicker basket, containing, among other luxuries and necessities, half a dozen bottles of claret, a segment of cheese, and some heads of lettuce; the whole surmounted by a clean leather-covered pass-book inscribed with the name and avenue number of the confiding and accommodating grocer who supplied the colonel's daily wants.

"De colonel an' Misser Fizpat'ic bofe waitin' for you, sah," said that obsequious darky, preceding me through the dark passage. I followed, mounted the old-fashioned wooden steps, and fell into the out-

stretched arms of the colonel before I could touch the knocker.

"Here he is, Fitz!" and the next instant I was sharing with that genial gentleman the warmth of the colonel's fire.

"Now then, Chad," called out the colonel, "take this lettuce and give it a dip in the snow for five minutes ; and here,

Chad, befo' you go hand me that claret.
Bless my soul! it is as cold as a dog's
nose; Fitz, set it on the mantel. And
hurry down to that mutton, Chad. Never
mind the basket. Leave it where it is."

Chad chuckled out to me as he closed
the door : "'Spec' I know mo' 'bout dat
saddle den de colonel. It ain't a-burnin'
none." And the colonel, satisfied now
that Chad's hand had reached the oven
door below, made a vigorous attack on the
blazing logs with the tongs, and sent a
flight of sparks scurrying up the chimney.

There was always a glow and breeze and
sparkle about the colonel's fire that I found
nowhere else. It partook to a certain extent of his personality — open, bright, and
with a great draft of enthusiasm always
rushing up a chimney of difficulties, buoyed
up with the hope of the broad clear of the
heaven of success above.

"My fire," he once said to me, " is my
friend ; and sometimes, my dear boy, when
you are all away and Chad is out, it seems
my only friend. After it talks to me for
hours we both get sleepy together, and I
cover it up with its gray blanket of ashes
and then go to bed myself. Ah, Major!

when you are gettin' old and have no wife
to love you and no children to make yo'
heart glad, a wood fire full of honest old
logs, every one of which is doing its best
to please you, is a great comfort."

"Draw closer, Major; vehy cold night,
gentlemen. We do not have any such
weather in my State. Fitz, have you
thawed out yet?"

Fitz looked up from a pile of documents
spread out on his lap, his round face aglow
with the firelight, and compared himself to
half a slice of toast well browned on both
sides.

"I am glad of it. I was worried about
you when you came in. You were chilled
through."

Then turning to me: "Fact is, Fitz is
a little overworked. Enormous strain, suh,
on a man solving the vast commercial prob-
lems that he is called upon to do every day."

After which outburst the colonel crossed
the room and finished unpacking the
basket, placing the cheese in one of the
empty plates on the table, and the various
other commodities on the sideboard. When
he reached the pass-book he straightened

himself up, held it off admiringly, turned the leaves slowly, his face lighting up at the goodly number of clean pages still between its covers, and said thoughtfully : —

"Very beautiful custom, this pass-book system, gentlemen, and quite new to me. One of the most co'teous attentions I have received since I have taken up my residence Nawth. See how simple it is. I send my servant to the sto' for my supplies. He returns in haalf an hour with everything I need, and brings back this book which I keep,—remember, gentlemen, which I *keep*, — a mark of confidence which in this degen'rate age is refreshin'. No vulgar bargainin', suh ; no disagreeable remarks about any former unsettled account. It certainly is delightful."

"When are the accounts under this system generally paid, Colonel," asked Fitz.

With the exception of a slight tremor around the corners of his mouth Fitz's face expressed nothing but the idlest interest.

"I have never inquired, suh, and would not hurt the gentleman's feelin's by doin' so for the world," he replied with dignity. "I presume, when the book is full."

Whatever might have been Fitz's mental workings, there was no mistaking the colonel's. He believed every word he said.

"What a dear old trump the colonel is," said Fitz, turning to me, his face wrinkling all over with suppressed laughter.

All this time Chad was passing in and out, bearing dishes and viands, and when all was ready and the table candles were lighted, he announced that fact softly to .his master and took his customary place behind his chair.

The colonel was as delightful as ever, his talk ranging from politics and family blood to possum hunts and modern literature, while the mutton and its accessories did full credit to Chad's culinary skill.

In fact the head of the colonel's table was his throne. Nowhere else was he so charming, and nowhere else did the many sides to his delightful nature give out such varied hues.

Fitz, practical business man as he was, would listen to his many schemes by the hour, charmed into silence and attentive appreciation by the sublime faith that sustained his host, and the perfect honesty and sincerity underlying everything he did.

But it was not until the cheese had completely lost its geometrical form, the coffee served, and the pipes lighted, that the subject which of all others absorbed him was broached. Indeed, it was a rule of the colonel's, never infringed upon, that, no matter how urgent the business, the dinner-hour was to be kept sacred.

"Salt yo' food, suh, with humor," he would say. "Season it with wit, and sprinkle it all over with the charm of good-fellowship, but never poison it with the cares of yo' life. It is an insult to yo' digestion, besides bein', suh, a mark of bad breedin'."

"Now, Major," began the colonel, turning to me, loosening the string around a package of papers, and spreading them out like a game of solitaire, "draw yo' chair closer. Fitz, hand me the map."

A diligent search revealed the fact that the map had been left at the office, and so the colonel proceeded without it, appealing now and then to Fitz, who leaned over his chair, his arm on the table.

"Befo' I touch upon the financial part of this enterprise, Major, let me show you where this road runs," said the colonel,

reaching for the casters. " I am sorry I
have n't the map, but we can get along
very well with this ; " and he unloaded the
cruets.

" This mustard-pot, here, is Caartersville, the startin' - point of our system.
This town, suh, has now a population of
mo' than fo' thousand people ; in five
years it will have fo'ty thousand. From
this point the line follows the bank of the
Big Tench River — marked by this caarvin' - knife — to this salt-cellar, where it
crosses its waters by an iron bridge of two
spans, each of two hundred and fifty feet.
Then, suh, it takes a sharp bend to the
southard and stops at my estate, the road-
bed skirtin' within a convenient distance
of Caarter Hall.

" Please move yo' arm, Fitz.   I have n't
room enough to lay out the city of Fairfax.
Thank you.

" Just here," continued the colonel, util-
izing the remains of the cheese, " is to be
the future city of Fairfax, named after my
ancestor, suh, General Thomas Wilmot
Fairfax of Somerset, England, who settled
here in 1680. From here we take a course
due nawth, stopping at Talcottville eight

miles, and thence nawthwesterly to Warrentown and the broad Atlantic ; in all
fifty miles."

"Any connecting road at Warrentown ?"
I asked.

"No, suh, nor anywhere else along the
line. It is absolutely virgin country, and
this is one of the strong points of the
scheme, for there can be no competition ; "
and the colonel leaned back in his chair,
and looked at me with the air of a man
who had just informed me of a legacy of
half a million of dollars and was watching
the effect of the news.

I preserved my gravity, and followed the
imaginary line with my eye, bounding
from the mustard-pot along the carving-
knife to the salt-cellar and back in a loop
to the cheese, and then asked if the Big
Tench could not be crossed higher up, and
if so why was it necessary to build twelve
additional miles of road.

"To reach Carter Hall," said Fitz quietly.

"Any advantage ? " I asked in perfect
good faith.

The colonel was on his feet in a moment.

"Any advantage ? Major, I am surprised at you! A place settled mo' than one hundred years ago, belongin' to one of the vehy fust fam'lies of Virginia, not to be of any advantage to a new enterprise like this! Why, suh, it will give an air of respectability to the whole thing that nothin' else could ever do. Leave out Caarter Hall, suh, and you pa'alize the whole scheme. Am I not right, Fitz ? "

"Unquestionably, Colonel. It is really all the life it has," replied Fitz, solemn as a graven image, blowing a cloud of smoke through his nose.

"And then, suh," continued the colonel with increasing enthusiasm, oblivious to the point of Fitz's remark, "see the improvements. Right here to the eastward of this cheese we shall build a round-house marked by this napkin-ring, which will accommodate twelve locomotives, construct extensive shops for repairs, and erect large foundries and caar-shops. Altogether, suh, we shall expend at this point mo' than — mo' than — one million of dollars ; " and the colonel threw back his head and gazed at the ceiling, his lips computing imaginary sums.

"Befo' these improvements are complete it will be necessary, of course, to take care of the enormous crowds that will flock in for a restin'-place. So to the left of this napkin-ring, on a slightly risin' ground, — just here where I raise the cloth, — is where the homes of the people will be erected. I have the refusal " — here the colonel lowered his voice — " of two thousand acres of the best private-residence land in the county, contiguous to this very spot, which I can buy for fo' dollars an acre. It is worth fo' dollars a square foot if it is worth a penny. But, suh, it would be little short of highway rob'ry to take this property at that figger, and I shall arrange with Fitz to include in his prospectus the payment of one hundred dollars an acre for this land, payable either in the common stock of our road or in the notes of the company, as the owners may elect."

"But, Colonel," said I, with a sincere desire to get at the facts, "where is the Golconda — the gold mine? Where do I come in ? "

"Patience, my dear Major; I am coming to that.

"Fitz, read that prospectus."

" I have," said Fitz, turning to the colonel, " somewhat modified your rough draft, to meet the requirements of our market ; but not materially.   Of course I cannot commit myself to any fixed earning capacity until I go over the ground, which we will do together shortly.   But " — raising the candle to the level of his nose — " this is as near as I can come to your ideas with any hopes of putting the loan through here.   I have, as you will see, left the title of the bond as you wished, although the issue is a novel one to our Exchange." Then turning to me : " This of course is only a preliminary announcement."

THE CARTERSVILLE AND WARRENTOWN AIR LINE RAILROAD.

THE GARDEN SPOT OF VIRGINIA SEEKS AN OUTLET TO THE SEA.

CAPITAL ONE MILLION OF DOLLARS, DIVIDED INTO

50,000 Founders' shares at . . . . $10.00 each
5,000 Ordinary   "   " . . . . 100.00 "

BONDED DEBT FOR PURPOSES OF CONSTRUCTION ONLY.

ONE MILLION OF DOLLARS
IN
1,000 FIRST MORTGAGE BONDS OF $1000.00 EACH.

FULL PROTECTION GUARANTEED.

The undersigned, Messrs. . . . . . . offer for
sale $500,000.00 of the 6% Deferred Debenture Bonds
of the C. & W. Air Line Railroad at par and accrued
interest, together with a limited amount of the ordinary
shares at 50%.

Subscription books close . . . .
Promoters reserve the right to advance prices without
further notice.

"There, Major, is a prospectus that
caarries conviction on its vehy face," said
the colonel, reaching for the document.

I complimented the eminent financier on
his skill, and was about to ask him what it
all meant, when the colonel, who had been
studying it carefully, broke in with : —

"Fitz, there is one thing you left out."

"Yes, I know, the name of the banker;
I have n't found him yet."

"No, Fitz; but the words, '*Subscrip-
tions opened Simultaneously in New York,
London, Richmond,*' and " —

"Cartersville?" suggested Fitz.

"Certainly, suh."

"Any money in Cartersville?"

"No, suh, not much; but we can *sub-scribe*, can't we? The name and influence of our leadin' citizens would give tone and dignity to any subscription list. Think of this, suh!" and the colonel traced imaginary inscriptions on the back of Fitz's prospectus with his forefinger, voicing them as he went on:—

The Hon. JOHN PAGE LOWNES,
    Member of the State Legislature . . 1,000 shares
The Hon. I. B. KERFOOT,
    Jedge of the District Court of
      Fairfax County . . . . 1,000 shares
Major THOMAS C. YANCEY,
    Late of the Confederate Army . . . 500 shares

"These gentlemen are my friends, suh, and would do anythin' to oblige me."

Fitz sharpened a lead pencil and without a word inserted the desired amendment.

The colonel studied the document for another brief moment and struck another snag.

"And, Fitz, what do you mean, by 'full protection guaranteed'?"

"To the bondholder, of course,—the man who pays the money."

" What kind of protection ? "

"Why, the right to foreclose the mortgage when the interest is not paid, of course," said Fitz, with a surprised look.

" Put yo' pencil through that line, quick —none of that for me. This fo'closure business has ruined haalf the gentlemen in our county, suh. But for that foolishness two thirds of our fust families would still be livin' in their homes. No, suh, strike it out ! "

" But, my dear Colonel, without that protecting clause you could n't get a banker to touch your bonds with a pair of tongs. What recourse have they ? "

" What reco'se ? Reorganization, suh! A boilin'-down process which will make the stock — which we practically give away at fifty cents on the dollar — twice as valuable. I appreciate, my dear Fitz, the effo'ts which you are makin' to dispose of these secu'ities, but you must remember that this plan is *mine*.

" Now Major," locking his arm in mine, "listen ; for I want you both to understand exactly the way in which I propose to forward this enterprise. Chad, bring me three wine-glasses and put that Ma-

deira on the table — don't disturb that railroad ! — so.

"My idea, gentlemen," continued the
colonel, filling the glasses himself, "is to
start this scheme honestly in the beginnin',
and avoid all dissatisfaction on the part of
these vehy bondholders thereafter.

"Now, suh, in my experience I have always discovered that a vehy general dissatisfaction is sure to manifest itself if the
coupons on secu'ities of this class are not
paid when they become due.   As a gen'ral
rule this interest money is never earned
for the fust two years, and the money to
pay it with is inva'ably stolen from the
principal.   All this dishonesty I avoid, suh,
by the issue of my Deferred Debenture
Bonds."

"How?" I asked, seeing the colonel
pause for a reply.

"By cuttin' off the fust fo' coupons.
Then everybody knows exactly where they
stand.   They don't expect anythin' and
they never get it."

Fitz gave one of his characteristic roars
and asked if the fifth would ever be paid.

"I can't at this moment answer, but we
hope it will."

"It is immaterial," said Fitz, wiping his eyes. "This class of purchasers are all speculators, and like excitement. The very uncertainty as to this fifth coupon gives interest to the investment, if not to the investor."

"None of yo' Irish impudence, suh. No, gentlemen, the plan is not only fair, but reasonable. Two years is not a long period of time in which to foster a great enterprise like the C. & W. A. L. R. R., and it is for this purpose that I issue the Deferred Debentures. Deferred — put off ; Debenture — owed. What we owe we put off. Simple, easily understood, and honest.

"Now, suh," turning to Fitz, "if after this frank statement any graspin' banker seeks to trammel this enterprise by any fo'closure clauses, he sha'n't have a bond, suh. I 'll take them all myself fust."

Fitz agreed to the striking out of all such harassing clauses, and the colonel continued his inspection.

"One mo' and I am done, Fitz. What do you mean by Founders' shares ?"

"Shares for the promoters and the first subscribers. They cost one tenth of the ordinary shares and draw five times as

much dividend. It is quite a popular form
of investment. They, of course, are not
sold until all the bonds are disposed of."

"How many of these Founders' shares
are there?"

"Fifty thousand at ten dollars each."

The colonel paused a moment and communed inwardly with himself.

"Put me down for twenty-five thousand,
Fitz. Part cash, and the balance in such
po'tion of my estate as will be required for
the purposes of the road."

The colonel did not specify the propor-
tions, but Fitz made a pencil memorandum
on the margin of the prospectus with the
same sort of respectful silence he would
have shown the Rothschilds in a similar
transaction, while the colonel refilled his
glass and held it between his nose and the
candle.

"And now, Major, what shall we reserve
for you?" said he, laying his hand on my
shoulder. Before I could reply Fitz raised
his finger, looked at me significantly over
the rims of his spectacles, and said : —

"With your permission, Colonel, the
Major and I will divide the remaining
twenty-five thousand between ourselves."

Then seeing my startled look, "I will give you ample notice, Major, before the first partial payment is called in."

"You overwhelm me, gentlemen," said the colonel, rising from his seat and seizing us by the hands. "It has been the dream of my life to have you both with me in this enterprise, but I had no idea it would be realized so soon. Fill yo' glasses and join me in a sentiment that is dear to me as my life, — 'The Garden Spot of Virginia in search of an Outlet to the Sea.'"

Nothing could have been more exhilarating than the colonel's manner after this. His enthusiasm became so contagious that I began to feel something like a millionaire myself, and to wonder whether this were not the opportunity of my life. Fitz was so far affected that he recanted to a certain extent his disbelief in the omission of the foreclosure clause, and even expressed himself as being hopeful of getting around it in some way.

As for the colonel, the railroad was to him already a fixed fact. He could really shut his eyes at any time and hear the whistle of the down train nearing the bridge over the Tench. Such trifling details as the finding of a banker who would attempt to negotiate the loan, the subsequent selling of the securities, and the minor items of right of way, construction, etc., were matters so light and trivial as not to cause him a moment's uneasiness. Cartersville was to him the centre of the earth, hampered and held back by lack of proper connections with the outlying portions of the universe. What mattered the rest?

"Make a memorandum, Fitz, to have me send for a bridge engineer fust thing after I get to my office in the mornin'. There will be some difficulty in gettin' a proper foundation for the centre-pier of that bridge, and some one should be sent at once to make a survey. We can't be delayed at this point a day. And, Fitz, while I think of it, there should be a wagon bridge at or near this iron structure, and the timber might as well be gotten out now. It will facilitate haulin' supplies into Fairfax city."

Fitz thought so too, and made a second memorandum to that effect, recording the suggestion very much as a private secretary would an order from his railroad magnate.

The colonel gave this last order with coat thrown open, — thumbs in his vest, — back to the fire, — an attitude never indulged in except on rare occasions, and then only when the very weight of the problem necessitated a corresponding bracing up, and more breathing room.

These attitudes, by the way, were very suggestive of the colonel's varying moods. Sometimes, when he came home, tired out with the hard pavements of the city, so different from the soft earth of his native roads, I would find him bunched up in his chair in the twilight; face in hands, elbows on knees, crooning over the fire, the silver streaks in his hair glistening in the flickering firelight, building castles in the glowing coals, — the old manor house restored and the barns rebuilt, the gates rehung, the old quarters repaired, the little negroes again around the doors; and he once more catching the sound of the yellow-painted coach on the gravel, with Chad helping the dear old aunt down the porch steps. This, deep down in the bottom of his soul, was really the dream and purpose of his life.

It never seemed nearer of realization

than now. The very thought suffused his whole being with a suppressed joy, visible in his face even when he began loosening the two lower buttons of his old thread-bare coat, throwing back the lapels and

slowly extending his fingers fan-like over his dilating chest.

I always knew what suddenly sweetened his smile from one of triumphant pride to one of tenderness.

"And the old home, Fitz, something must be done there; we must receive our friends properly."

Fitz agreed to everything, offering an amendment here, and a suggestion there, until our host's enthusiasm reached fever heat.

It was nearly midnight before the colonel had confided to Fitz all the pressing necessities of the coming day. Even then he followed us both to the door, with parting instructions to Fitz, saying over and over again that it had been the happiest night of his life. And he would have gone bare-headed to the outer gate had not Chad caught him half way down the steps, thrown a coat over his head and shoulders, and gently led him back with : —

"'Clar to goodness, Marsa George, what kind foolishness dis yer? Is you tryin' to ketch yo' death?"

Once on the outside and the gate shut, Fitz's whole manner changed. He became suddenly thoughtful, and did not speak until we reached the tall clock tower with its full moon of a face shining high up against the black winter night.

Then he stood still, looked out over the white street, dotted here and there with belated wayfarers trudging home through the snow, and said with a tremor in his voice which startled me : —

"I could n't raise a dollar in a lunatic asylum full of millionaires on a scheme like the colonel's, and yet I keep on lying to the dear old fellow day after day, hoping that something will turn up by which I can help him out."

"Then tell him so."

Fitz laid his hand on my shoulder, looked me straight in the face, and said: —

"I cannot.   It would break his heart."

CHAPTER III

An Old Family Servant

THE colonel's front yard, while as quaint
and old-fashioned as his house, was not —
if I may be allowed — quite so well bred.

This came partly from the outdoor life
it had always led and from its close asso-
ciation with other yards that had lost all
semblance of respectability, and partly
from the fact that it had never felt the
refining influences of the friends of the
house; for nobody ever lingered in the
front yard who by any possibility could
get into the front door — nobody, except
perhaps now and then a stray tramp, who
felt at home at once and went to sleep on
the steps.

That all this told upon its character and
appearance was shown in the remnants of
whitewash on the high wall, scaling off in
discolored patches; in the stagger of the
tall fence opposite, drooping like a drunk-
ard between two policemen of posts; and

in the unkempt, bulging rear of the third
wall, — the front house, — stuffed with
rags and tied up with clothes-lines.

If in the purity of its youth it had ever
seen better days as a garden — but then
no possible stretch of imagination, however
brilliant, could ever convert this miserable
quadrangle into a garden.

It contained, of course, as all such yards
do, one lone plant, — this time a honeysuckle, — which had clambered over the
front door and there rested as if content to
stay ; but which later on, frightened at the
surroundings, had with one great spring
cleared the slippery wall between, reached
the rain-spout above, and by its helping
arm had thus escaped to the roof and the
sunlight.

It is also true that high up on this same
wall there still clung the remains of a criss-
cross wooden trellis supporting the shiver-
ing branches of an old vine, which had
spent its whole life trying to grow high
enough to look over the tall fence into the
yard beyond ; but this was so long ago
that not even the landlord remembered the
color of its blossoms.

Then there was an old-fashioned hy-

drant, with a half-spiral crank of a handle
on its top and the curved end of a lead
pipe always aleak thrust through its rotten
side, with its little statues of ice all winter
and its spattering slop all summer.

Besides all this there were some broken
flower-pots in a heap in one corner, — sui-
cides from the window-sills above, — and
some sagging clothes-lines, and a battered
watering-pot, and a box or two that might
once have held flowers; and yet with all
this circumstantial evidence against me I
cannot conscientiously believe that this
forlorn courtyard ever could have risen to
the dignity of a garden.

But of course nothing of all this can be
seen at night. At night one sees only the
tall clock tower of Jefferson Market with
its one blazing eye glaring high up over
the fence, the little lantern hung in the
tunnel, and the glow through the curtains
shading the old-fashioned windows of the
house itself, telling of warmth and comfort
within.

To-night when I pushed open the swinging door — the door of the tunnel entering
from the street — the lantern was gone,
and in its stead there was only the glim-

mer of a mysterious light moving about the yard, — a light that fell now on the bare wall, now on the front steps, making threads of gold of the twisted iron railings, then on the posts of the leaning fence, against which hung three feathery objects, — grotesque and curious in the changing shadows, — and again on some barrels and boxes surrounded by loose straw.

Following this light, in fact, guiding it, was a noiseless, crouching figure peering under the open steps, groping around the front door, creeping beneath the windows; moving uneasily with a burglar-like tread.

I grasped my umbrella, advanced to the edge of the tunnel, and called out : —

" Who 's that ? "

The figure stopped, straightened up, held a lantern high over its head, and peered into the darkness.

There was no mistaking that face.

" Oh, that 's you, Chad, is it ? What the devil are you doing ? "

" Lookin' for one ob dese yer tar'pins Miss Nancy sent de colonel. Dey was seben ob 'em in dis box, an' now dey ain't but six. Hole dis light, Major, an' lemme fumble round dis rain-spout."

Chad handed me the lantern, fell on his
knees, and began crawling around the

small yard like an old dog hunting for a
possum, feeling in among the roots of the

honeysuckle, between the barrels that had brought the colonel's china from Carter Hall, under the steps, way back where Chad kept his wood ashes — but no " brer tar'pin."

" Well, if dat don't beat de lan' ! Dey was two ba'els — one had dat wild turkey an' de pair o' geese you see hangin' on de fence dar, an' de udder ba'el I jest ca'aed down de cellar full er oishters. De tar'pins was in dis box — seben ob 'em. Spec' dat rapscallion crawled ober de fence ? " And Chad picked up the basket with the remaining half dozen, and descended the basement steps on his way through the kitchen to the front door above. Before he reached the bottom step I heard him break out with : —

" Oh, yer you is, you black debbil ! Tryin' to git in de door, is ye ? De pot is whar you 'll git ! "

At the foot of the short steps, flat on his back, head and legs wriggling like an overturned roach, lay the missing terrapin. It had crawled to the edge of the opening and had fallen down in the darkness.

Chad picked him up and kept on grumbling, shaking his finger at the motionless terrapin, whose head and legs were now tight drawn between its shells.

"Gre't mine to squash ye! Wearin' out my old knees lookin' for ye. Nebber mine, I 'm gwine to bile ye fust an' de longest — hear dat? — de longest!" Then looking up at me, "I got him, Major — try dat do'. Spec' it's open. Colonel ain't yer yit. Reckon some ob dem moonshiners is keepin' him down town. 'Fo' I forgit it, dar's a letter for ye hangin' to de mantelpiece."

The door and the letter were both open, the latter being half a sheet of paper impaled by a pin, which alone saved it from the roaring fire that Chad had just replenished.

I held it to the light and learned, to my disappointment, that business of enormous importance to the C. & W. A. L. R. R. might preclude the possibility of the colonel's leaving his office until late. If such a calamity overtook him, would I forgive him and take possession of his house and cellar and make myself as comfortable as I could with my best friend away? This postscript followed: —

"Open the new Madeira; Chad has the key."

Chad wreaked his vengeance upon the absconding terrapin by plunging him, with all his sins upon him, headlong into the boiling pot, and half an hour later was engaged at a side table in removing, with the help of an iron fork, the upper shell of the steaming vagabond, for my special comfort and sustenance.

" Tar'pin jes like a crab, Major, on'y got mo' meat to 'em. But you got to know 'em fust to eat 'em. Now dis yer shell is de hot plate, an' ye do all yo' eatin' right inside it," said Chad, dropping a spoonful of butter, the juice of a lemon, and a pinch of salt into the impromptu dish.

" Now, Major, take yo' fork an' pick out all dat black meat an' dip it in de sauce, an' wid ebery mou'ful take one o' dem little yaller eggs. Dat 's de way *we* eat tar'-pin. Dis yer stewin' him up in pote wine is scand'lous. Can't taste nuffin' but de wine. But dat 's *tar'pin.*"

I followed Chad's directions to the word, picking the terrapin as I would a crab and smothering the dainty bits in the hot sauce, until only two empty shells and a heap of little bones were left to tell the tale of my appetite.

"Gwine to crawl ober de fence, was ye?"
I heard him say with a chuckle as he bore
away the débris. "What I tell ye? Whar
am ye now?"

"Did Miss Nancy send those terrapin?"
I asked, watching the old darky drawing
the cork of the new Madeira referred to in
the colonel's note.

"Ob co'se, Major; Miss Nancy gibs de
colonel eberytin'. Did n't ye know dat?
She's de on'y one what's got anythin' to
gib, an' she would n't hab dat on'y frough
de war her money was in de bank in Bal-
timo'. I know, 'cause I went dar once to
git some for her. De Yankee soldiers
searched me; but some possums got two
holes."

"And did she send him the Madeira
too?"

"No, sah; Mister Grocerman gib him
dat."

As he pronounced this name his voice
fell, and for some time thereafter he kept
silent, brushing the crumbs away, replacing
a plate or two, or filling my wine-glass, until at last he took his place behind my chair
as was his custom with his master. It was
easy to see that Chad had something on
his mind.

Every now and then a sigh escaped him,
which he tried to conceal by some irrele-
vant remark, as if his sorrow were his own
and not to be shared with a stranger.   Finally he gave an uneasy glance around,
and, looking into my face with an expression of positive pain, said : —

"Don't tell de colonel I axed, but when
is dis yer railroad gwineter fotch some
money in ?"

"Why?" said I, wondering what extrav-
agance the old man had fallen into.

"Nuffin', sah ; but if it don't putty quick
dar's gwineter be trouble.   Dese yer gemmen on de av'nue is gittin' ugly.   When I
got dar Madary de udder day de tall one
warn't gwineter gib it to me, pass-book or
no pass-book.   On'y de young one say
he'd seen de colonel, an' he was a gemmen an' all right, I would n't 'a' got it at
all.   De tall gemmen was comin' right
around hisself — what he wanted to see,
he said, was de color ob de colonel's
money.   Been mo' den two months, an'
not a cent.

"Co'se I tole same as I been tellin' him,
dat de colonel's folks is quality folks ; but
he say dat don't pay de bills."

" Did you tell the colonel ? "

" No, sah ; ain't no use tellin' de colonel ; on'y worry him. He's got de pass-
book, but I ain't yerd him say nuffin' yit
'bout payin' him. I been spectin' Miss
Nancy up here, an' de colonel says she's
comin' putty soon. She'll fix 'em ; but
dey ain't no time to waste."

While he spoke there came a loud knock
at the door, and Chad returned trembling
with fear, his face the very picture of despair.

" Dat's de tall man hisself, sah, an' his
dander's up. I knowed dese Yankees in
de war, an' I don't like 'em when dey's ris'.
When I tole him de colonel ain't home he
look at me pizen-like, same as I was a-lyin' ;
an' den he stop an' listen an' say he come
back to-night. Trouble comin' ; old coon
smells de dog. Wish we was home an' out
ob dis ! "

I tried to divert his attention into other
channels and to calm his fears, assuring
him that the colonel would come out all
right ; that these enterprises were slow,
etc. ; but the old man only shook his head.

" You know, Major, same as me, dat de
colonel ain't nuffin' but a chile, an' about

his bills he 's *wuss.* But I 'm yer, an' I 'm
'sponsible. 'Chad,' he says, 'go out an'
git six mo' bottles of dat old Madary ;' an'
'Chad, don't forgit de sweet ile ;' an'
'Chad, is we got claret enough to last ober
Sunday ?' — an' not a cent in de house. I
ain't slep' none for two nights, worritin'
ober dis business, an' I 'm mos' crazy."

I laid down my knife and fork and looked
up. The old man's lip was quivering, and
something very like a tear stood in each
eye.

"I can't hab nuffin' happen to de fambly, Major. You know our folks is quality,
an' always was, an' I dassent look my mistress in de face if anythin' teches Marsa
George." Then bending down he said in
a hoarse whisper : "See dat old clock out
dar wid his eye wide open ? Know what
's down below dat in de cellar ? De jail !"
And two tears rolled down his cheeks.

It was some time before I could quiet
the old man's anxieties and coax him back
into his usual good humor, and then only
when I began to ask him of the old plantation days.

Then he fell to talking about the colo-

nel's father, Gen-
eral John Carter,
and the high days
at Carter Hall
when Miss Nan-
cy was a young
lady and the colo-
nel a boy home
from the univer-
sity.

"Dem was high
times. We ain't
neber seed no
time like dat
since de war. Git
up in de mawnin'
an' look out ober
de lawn, an' yer
come fo'teen or fifteen couples ob de fust-
est quality folks, all on horseback ridin' in
de gate. Den such a scufflin' round! Old
marsa an' missis out on de po'ch, an' de little pickaninnies runnin' from de quarters,
an' all hands helpin' 'em off de horses, an'
dey all smokin' hot wid de gallop up de
lane.

"An' den sich a breakfast an' sich dan-
cin' an' co'tin'; ladies all out on de lawn in

der white dresses, an' de gemmen in fair-
top boots, an' Mammy Jane runnin' round
same as a chicken wid its head off, — an'
der heads was off befo' dey knowed it, an'
dey a-br'ilin' on de gridiron.

"Dat would go on a week or mo', an' den
up dey'll all git an' away dey'd go to de
nex' plantation, an' take Miss Nancy along
wid 'em on her little sorrel mare, an' I on
Marsa John's black horse, to take care bofe
of 'em.   Dem *was* times!

"My old marsa," — and his eyes glistened, — "my old Marsa John was a gemman, sah, like dey don't see nowadays. Tall,
sah, an' straight as a cornstalk; hair white
an' silky as de tassel; an' a voice like de
birds was singin', it was dat sweet.

"'Chad,' he use' ter say, — you know I
was young den, an' I was his body servant,
— 'Chad, come yer till I bre'k yo' head;'
an' den when I come he'd laugh fit to kill
hisself. Dat's when you do right. But
when you was a low-down nigger an' got
de debbil in yer, an' ole marsa hear it an'
send de oberseer to de quarters for you to
come to de little room in de big house whar
de walls was all books an' whar his desk
was, 't wa'n't no birds about his voice den,
— mo' like de thunder."

"Did he whip his negroes?"

"No, sah; don't reckelmember a single lick laid on airy nigger dat de marsa knowed of; but when dey got so bad — an' some niggers is dat way — den dey was sold to de swamp lan's. He would n't hab 'em round 'ruptin' his niggers, he use' ter say.

"Hab coffee, sah? Won't take I a minute to bile it. Colonel ain't been drinkin' none lately, an' so I don't make none."

I nodded my head, and Chad closed the door softly, taking with him a small cup and saucer, and returning in a few minutes followed by that most delicious of all aromas, the savory steam of boiling coffee.

"My Marsa John," he continued, filling the cup with the smoking beverage, "never drank nuffin' but tea, eben at de big dinners when all de gemmen had coffee in de little cups — dat 's one ob 'em you 's drinkin' out ob now; dey ain't mo' dan fo' on 'em left. Old marsa would have his pot ob tea: Henny use' ter make it for him; makes it now for Miss Nancy.

"Henny was a young gal den, long 'fo' we was married. Henny b'longed to Colonel Lloyd Barbour, on de next plantation to ourn.

"Mo' coffee, Major?" I handed Chad the empty cup. He refilled it, and went straight on without drawing breath.

"Wust scrape I eber got into wid old Marsa John was ober Henny. I tell ye she was a harricane in dem days. She come into de kitchen one time where I was helpin' git de dinner ready an' de cook had gone to de spring house, an' she says : —

"'Chad, what ye cookin' dat smells so nice?'

"'Dat's a goose,' I says, 'cookin' for Marsa John's dinner. We got quality,' says I, pointin' to de dinin'-room do'.

"'Quality!' she says. 'Spec' I know what de quality is. Dat's for you an' de cook.'

"Wid dat she grabs a caarvin' knife from de table, opens de do' ob de big oven, cuts off a leg ob de goose, an' dis'pears round de kitchen corner wid de leg in her mouf.

"'Fo' I knowed whar I was Marsa John come to de kitchen do' an' says, 'Gittin' late, Chad ; bring in de dinner.' You see, Major, dey ain't no up an' down stairs in de big house, like it is yer ; kitchen an' dinin'-room all on de same flo'.

"Well, sah, I was scared to def, but I

tuk dat goose an' laid him wid de cut side
down on de bottom of de pan 'fo' de cook
got back, put some dressin' an' stuffin' ober
him, an' shet de stove do'. Den I tuk de
sweet potatoes an' de hominy an' put 'em
on de table, an' den I went back in de
kitchen to git de baked ham. I put on de
ham an' some mo' dishes, an' marsa says,
lookin' up : —

" ' I t'ought dere was a roast goose,
Chad ? '

" ' I ain't yerd nothin' 'bout no goose,' I
says. ' I 'll ask de cook.'

" Next minute I yerd old marsa a-holler-
in' : —

" ' Mammy Jane, ain't we got a goose ? '

" ' Lord-a-massy ! yes, marsa. Chad, you
wu'thless nigger, ain't you tuk dat goose
out yit ? '

" ' Is we got a goose ? ' said I.

" ' *Is we got a goose ?* Did n't you help
pick it ? '

" I see whar my hair was short, an' I
snatched up a hot dish from de hearth,
opened de oven do', an' slide de goose in
jes as he was, an' lay him down befo' Marsa
John.

" ' Now see what de ladies 'll have for

dinner,' says old marsa, pickin' up his caarvin' knife.

"'What 'll you take for dinner, miss?'
says I. 'Baked ham?'

"'No,' she says, lookin' up to whar
Marsa John sat; 'I think I 'll take a leg
ob dat goose'--jes so.

"Well, marsa cut off de leg an' put a little stuffin' an' gravy on wid a spoon, an'
says to me, 'Chad, see what dat gemman
'll have.'

"'What 'll you take for dinner, sah?'
says I. 'Nice breast o' goose, or slice o'
ham?'

"'No; I think I 'll take a leg of dat
goose,' he says.

"I did n't say nuffin', but I knowed bery
well he wa'n't a-gwine to git it.

"But, Major, you oughter seen ole marsa
lookin' for der udder leg ob dat goose! He
rolled him ober on de dish, dis way an' dat
way, an' den he jabbed dat ole bone-han-
dled caarvin' fork in him an' hel' him up
ober de dish an' looked under him an' on
top ob him, an' den he says, kinder sad
like:--

"'Chad, whar is de udder leg ob dat
goose?'

" 'It did n't hab none,' says I.

" ' You mean ter say, Chad, dat de gooses on my plantation on'y got one leg?'

" 'Some ob 'em has an' some ob 'em ain't. You see, marsa, we got two kinds in de pond, an' we was a little boddered to-day, so Mammy Jane cooked dis one 'cause I cotched it fust.'

" 'Well,' said he, lookin' like he look when he send for you in de little room, 'I 'll settle wid ye after dinner.'

" Well, dar I was shiverin' an' shakin' in my shoes, an' droppin' gravy an' spillin' de wine on de table-cloth, I was dat shuck up; an' when de dinner was ober he calls all de ladies an' gemmen, an' says, 'Now come down to de duck pond. I 'm gwineter show dis nigger dat all de gooses on my plantation got mo' den one leg.'

" I followed 'long, trapesin' after de whole kit an' b'ilin', an' when we got to de pond " — here Chad nearly went into a convulsion with suppressed laughter — " dar was de gooses sittin' on a log in de middle of dat ole green goose-pond wid one leg stuck down — so — an' de udder tucked under de wing."

Chad was now on one leg, balancing himself by my chair, the tears running down his cheeks.

" 'Dar, marsa,' says I, 'don't ye see? Look at dat ole gray goose! Dat 's de berry match ob de one we had to-day.'

" Den de ladies all hollered an' de gemmen laughed so loud dey yerd 'em at de big house.

" 'Stop, you black scoun'rel!' Marsa John says, his face gittin' white an' he a-jerkin' his handkerchief from his pocket. 'Shoo!'

" Major, I hope to have my brains kicked out by a lame grasshopper if ebery one ob dem gooses did n't put down de udder leg!

" 'Now, you lyin' nigger,' he says, raisin' his cane ober my head, 'I 'll show you ' —

" 'Stop, Marsa John!' I hollered; ''t ain't fair, 't ain't fair.'

" 'Why ain't it fair?' says he.

" ' 'Cause,' says I, 'you did n't say "Shoo!" to de goose what was on de table.' " [1]

[1] This story, and the story of the " Postmaster " in a preceding chapter, I have told for so many years and to so many people, and with such varied amplifications, that I have long since persuaded myself that they are crea-

Chad laughed until he choked.

" And did he thrash you ? "

"Marsa John ? No, sah. He laughed loud as anybody ; an' den dat night he says to me as I was puttin' some wood on de fire : —

" 'Chad, where did dat leg go ? ' An' so I ups an' tells him all about Henny, an' how I was lyin' 'cause I was 'feared de gal would git hurt, an' how she was on'y a-foolin', thinkin' it was my goose ; an' den de ole marsa look in de fire for a long time, an' den he says : —

" 'Dat 's Colonel Barbour's Henny, ain't it, Chad ? '

" 'Yes,' marsa, says I.

"Well, de next mawnin' he had his black horse saddled, an' I held the stirrup for him to git on, an' he rode ober to de Barbour plantation, an' did n't come back till plumb black night. When he come up I held de lantern so I could see his face, for I wa'n't easy in my mine all day. But it was all bright an' shinin' same as a' angel's.

tions of my own. I surmise, however, that the basis of the " Postmaster " can be found in the corner of some forgotten newspaper, and I know that the " One-Legged Goose " is as old as the " Decameron."

" 'Chad,' he says, handin' me de reins, 'I bought yo' Henny dis arternoon from Colonel Barbour, an' she 's comin' ober to-morrow, an' you can bofe git married next Sunday.' "

A cheerful voice at the yard door, and the next moment the colonel was stamping his feet on the hall mat, his first word to Chad an inquiry after my comfort, and his second an apology to me for what he called his brutal want of hospitality.

"But I could n't help it, Major. I had some letters, suh, that could not be postponed. Has Chad taken good care of you? No dinner, Chad; I dined down town. How is the Madeira, Major?"

I expressed my entire approbation of the wine, and was about to fill the colonel's glass when Chad leaned over with the same anxious look in his face.

"De grocerman was here, Colonel, an' lef' word dat he was comin' agin later."

"You don't say so, Chad, and I was out: most unfortunate occurrence! When he calls again show him in at once. It will give me great pleasure to see him."

Then turning to me, his mind on the

passbook and its empty pages, — "I'll lay a wager, Major, that man's father was a gentleman. The fact is, I have not treated him with proper respect. He has shown me every courtesy since I have been here, and I am ashamed to say that I have not once entered his doors. His calling twice in one evening touches me deeply. I did not expect to find yo' tradespeople so polite."

Chad's face was a study while his master spoke, but he was too well trained, and still too anxious over the outcome of the expected interview, to do more than bow obsequiously to the colonel, — his invariable custom when receiving an order, — and to close the door behind him.

"That old servant," continued the colonel, watching Chad leave the room, and drawing his chair nearer the fire, "has been in my fam'ly ever since he was bawn. But for him and his old wife, Mammy Henny, I would be homeless to-night." And then the colonel, with that soft cadence in his voice which I always noticed when he spoke of something that touched his heart, told me with evident feeling how, in every crisis of fire, pillage, and

raid, these two faithful souls had kept un-
ceasing watch about the old house ; refast-
ening the wrenched doors, replacing the
shattered shutters, or extinguishing the em-
bers of abandoned bivouac fires. Indeed,
for months at a time they were its only occupants, outside of strolling marauders and
bands of foragers, and but for their untir-
ing devotion its tall chimneys would long
since have stood like tombstones over the
grave of its ashes. Then he added, with a
break in his voice that told how deeply he
felt it : —

"Do you know, Major, that when I
was a prisoner at City Point that darky
tramped a hundred miles through the coast
swamps to reach me, crossed both lines
twice, hung around for three months for
his chance, and has carried in his leg ever
since the ball intended for me the night I
escaped in his clothes, and he was shot in
mine.

"I tell you, suh, the color of a man's skin
don't make much diffe'ence sometimes.
Chad was bawn a gentleman, and he'll
never get over it."

As he was speaking, the object of his
eulogy opened the hall door, and the next

instant a tall, red-headed man with closely
trimmed side-whiskers, and wearing a brown
check suit and a blue necktie, ran the gaunt-
let of Chad's profound but anxious bow,
and advanced towards the colonel, hat in
hand.

"Which is Mr. Carter?"

The colonel arose gracefully. "I am
Colonel Caarter, suh, and I presume you
are the gentleman to whom I am indebted
for so many courtesies. My servant tells
me that you called earlier in the evenin'.
I regret, suh, that I was detained so late
at my office, and I have to thank you for
perseve'in' the second time. I assure you,
suh, that I esteem it a special honor."

The tall gentleman with the auburn
whiskers wiped his face with a handkerchief, which he took from his hat, and
stated with some timidity that he hoped
he did not intrude at that late hour. He
had sent his pass-book, and —

"I have looked it over, suh, repeatedly,
with the greatest pleasure. It is a custom
new to us in my county, but it meets
with my hearty approval. Give yo' hat to
my servant, suh, and take this seat by the
fire."

The proprietor of the hat after some
protestations suffered Chad to bear away
that grateful protection to his slightly bald
head, — retaining his handkerchief, which
he finally rolled up into a little wad and
kept tightly clenched in the perspiring palm
of his left hand, — and then threw out the
additional hope that everything was satis-
factory.

"Delicious, suh ; I have not tasted such
Madeira since the wah. In my cellar at
home, suh, I once had some old Madeira
of '28 that was given to my father, the late
General John Caarter, by old Judge Thorn-
ton. You, of course, know that wine, suh.
Ah ! I see that you do."

And then followed one of the colonel's
delightful monologues descriptive of all
the vintages of that year, the colonel constantly appealing to the dazed and de-
lighted groceryman to be set right in minor
technical matters, — the grocer under-
standing them as little as he did the Az-
tec dialects, — the colonel himself supplying the needed data and then thanking
the auburn gentleman for the information
so charmingly that for the moment that
worthy tradesman began to wonder why he

had not long before risen from the com-
monplace level of canned vegetables to the
more sublime plane of wines in the wood.

"Now the Madeira you sent me this
mornin', suh, is a trifle too fruity for my
taste. Chad, open a fresh bottle."

The owner of the pass-book instantly
detected a very decided fruity flavor, but
thought he had another wine, which he
would send in the morning, that might
suit the colonel's palate better.

The colonel thanked him, and then
drifted into the wider field of domestic
delicacies, — the preserving of fruits, the
making of pickles as practiced on the plan-
tations by the old Virginia cooks, — the
colonel waxing eloquent over each produc-
tion, and the future wine merchant becoming more and more enchanted as the colonel flowed on.

When he rose to go the grocer had a
mental list of the things he would send
the colonel in the morning all arranged in
his commercial head, and so great was his
delight that, after shaking hands with me
once and with the colonel three times, he
would also have extended that courtesy to
Chad had not that perfectly trained servant

checkmated him by filling his extended palm with the rim of his own hat.

When Chad returned from bowing him

through the tunnel, the lines in his face a tangle of emotions, the colonel was standing on the mat, in his favorite attitude — back to the fire, coat thrown open, thumbs in his armholes, his outstretched fingers beating woodpecker tattoos on his vest.

Somehow the visit of the grocer had lifted him out of the cares of the day. How, he could not tell. Perhaps it was the fragrance of the Madeira; perhaps the respectful, overawed bow, — the bow of the tradesman the world over to the landed proprietor, — restoring to him for one brief moment that old feudal supremacy which above all else his soul loved. Perhaps it was only the warmth and cheer and comfort of it all.

Whatever it was, it buoyed and strengthened him. He was again in the old dining-hall at home : the servants moving noiselessly about ; the cut-glass decanters reflected in the polished mahogany ; the candles lighted ; his old, white-haired father, in his high-backed chair, sipping his wine from the slender glass.

Ah, the proud estate of the old plantation days ! Would they ever be his again ?

CHAPTER IV

The Arrival of a True Southern Lady

"MISTRESS yer, sah! Come yistidd'y mawnin'."

How Chad beamed all over when this simple statement fell from his lips!

I had not seen him since the night when he stood behind my chair and with bated breath whispered his anxieties lest the second advent of "de grocerman" should bring dire destruction to the colonel's household.

To-day he looked ten years younger. His kinky gray hair, generally knotted into little wads, was now divided by a well-defined path starting from the great wrinkle in his forehead and ending in a dense tangle of underbrush that no comb dared penetrate. His face glistened all over. His mouth was wide open, showing a great cavity in which each tooth seemed to dance with delight. His jacket was as white and stiff as soap and starch could make it, while

a cast-off cravat of the colonel's — double
starched to suit Chad's own ideas of propriety — was tied in a single knot, the two
ends reaching to the very edge of each ear.
To crown all, a red carnation flamed away
on the lapel of his jacket, just above an
outside pocket, which held in check a pair
of white cotton gloves bulging with importance and eager for use. Every time
he bowed he touched with a sweep both
sides of the narrow hall.

It was the first time in some weeks that
I had seen the interior of the colonel's
cozy dining-room by daylight. Of late my
visits had been made after dark, with drawn
curtains, lighted candles, and roaring wood
fires. But this time it was in the morning, — and a bright, sunny, lovely spring
morning at that, — with one window open
in the L and the curtains drawn back from
the other ; with the honeysuckle beginning to bud, its long runners twisting
themselves inquiringly through the half-
closed shutters as if anxious to discover
what all this bustle inside was about.

It was easy to see that some other touch
besides that of the colonel and his faithful
man-of-all-work had left its impress in the

bachelor apartment. There was a general air of order apparent. The irregular line of foot gear which decorated the wash-board of one wall, beginning with a pair of worsted slippers and ending with a wooden bootjack, was gone. Whisk-brooms and dusters that had never known a restful nail since they entered the colonel's ser-vice were now suspended peacefully on convenient hooks. Dainty white curtains, gathered like a child's frock, flapped lazily against the broken green blinds, while some sprays of arbutus, plucked by Miss Nancy on her way to the railroad station, drooped about a tall glass on the mantel.

Chad had solved the mystery, — Aunt Nancy came yesterday.

I found the table set for four, its chief feature being a tray bearing a heap of egg-shell cups and saucers I had not seen be-fore, and an old-fashioned tea-urn hum-ming a tune all to itself.

"De colonel's out, but he comin' back d'rektly," Chad said eagerly, all out of breath with excitement. Then followed the information that Mr. Fitzpatrick was coming to breakfast, and that he was to tell Miss Nancy the moment we arrived.

He then reduced the bulge in his outside
pocket by thrusting his big hands into his
white gloves, gave a sidelong glance at the
flower in his buttonhole, and bore my card
aloft with the air of a cupbearer serving a
princess.

A soft step on the stair, the rustle of
silk, a warning word outside : " Look out
for dat lower step, mistress — dat 's it ; "
and Miss Nancy entered the room.

No, I am wrong. She became a part of
it ; as much so as the old andirons and the
easy chairs and the old-fashioned mantel-
pieces, the snowy curtains and the trailing
vine. More so when she gave me the
slightest dip of a courtesy and laid her
dainty, wrinkled little hand in mine, and
said in the sweetest possible voice how
glad she was to see me after so many years,
and how grateful she felt for all my kind-
ness to the dear colonel. Then she sank
into a quaint rocking-chair that Chad had
brought down behind her, rested her feet
on a low stool that mysteriously appeared
from under the table, and took her knitting
from her reticule.

She had changed somewhat since I last
saw her, but only as would an old bit of

precious stuff that grew the more mellow
and harmonious in tone as it grew the
older. She had the same silky gray hair —
a trifle whiter, perhaps ; the same frank, ten-
der mouth, winning wherever she smiled ;
the same slight, graceful figure ; and the
same manner — its very simplicity a reflex
of that refined and quiet life she had always led. For hers had been an isolated
life, buried since her girlhood in a great
house far away from the broadening influences of a city, and saddened by the daily
witness of a slow decay of all she had been
taught to revere. But it had been a life so
filled with the largeness of generous deeds
that its returns had brought her the love
and reverence of every living soul she
knew.

While she sat and talked to me of her
journey I had time to enjoy again the
quaintness of her dress, — the quaintness
of forty years before. There was the same
old-fashioned, soft gray silk with up-and-
down stripes spotted with sprigs of flowers, the lace cap with its frill of narrow
pink ribbons and two wide pink strings
that fell over the shoulders, and the handkerchief of India mull folded across the

breast and fastened with an amethyst pin.
Her little bits of feet — they were literally
so — were incased in white stockings and
heelless morocco slippers bound with braid.

But her dress was never sombre. She
always seemed to remember, even in her
bright ribbons and silks, the days of her
girlhood, when half the young men in the
county were wild about her. When she
moved she wafted towards you a perfume
of sweet lavender — the very smell that you
remember came from your own mother's
old-fashioned bureau drawer when she let
you stand on tiptoe to see her pretty things.
When you kissed her — and once I did —
her cheek was as soft as a child's and fra-
grant with rose-water.

But I hear the colonel's voice outside,
laughing with Fitz.

"Come in, suh, and see the dearest
woman in the world."

The next instant he burst in dressed in
his gala combination, — white waistcoat
and cravat, the old coat thrown wide open
as if to welcome the world, and a bunch of
red roses in his hand.

"Nancy, here's my dear friend Fitz,
whom I have told you about, — the most

extraord'nary man of modern times. Ah,
Major! you here? Came in early, did you,
so as to have aunt Nancy all to yo'self?
Sit down, Fitz, right alongside of her."
And he kissed her hand gallantly. "Isn't
she the most delightful bit of old porcelain
you ever saw in all yo' bawn days?"

Miss Nancy rose, made another of her
graceful courtesies, and begged that neither
of us would mind the colonel's raillery;
she never could keep him in order. And
she laughed softly as she gave her hand to
Fitz, who touched it very much as if he
quite believed the colonel's reference to
the porcelain to be true.

"There you go, Nancy, 'busin' me like
a dog, and here I've been a-trampin' the
streets for a' hour lookin' for flowers for
you! You are breakin' my heart, Miss
Caarter, with yo' coldness and contempt.
Another word and you shall not have a single bud." And the colonel gayly tucked a
rose under her chin with a loving stroke
of his hand, and threw the others in a heap
on her lap.

"Breakfast sarved, mistress," said Chad
in a low voice.

The colonel gave his arm to his aunt

with the air of a courtier ; Fitz and I disposed ourselves on each side ; Chad, with
reverential mien, screwed his eyes up tight ;
and the colonel said grace with an increased
fervor in his voice, no doubt remembering
in his heart the blessing of the last arrival.

Throughout the entire repast the colonel
was in his gayest mood, brimming over
with anecdotes and personal reminiscences
and full of his rose-colored plans for the
future.

Many things had combined to produce
this happy frame of mind. There was first
the Scheme, which had languished for
weeks owing to the vise-like condition of
the money market, — another of Fitz's
mendacious excuses, — and which had now
been suddenly galvanized into temporary
life by an inquiry made by certain bankers
who were seeking an outlet for English
capital, and who had expressed a desire to
investigate the " Garden Spot of Virginia."
Only an " inquiry," but to the colonel the
papers were already signed. Then there
was the arrival of his distinguished guest,
whom he loved devotedly and with a certain old-school gallantry and tenderness as

picturesque as it was interesting. Last of
all there was that important episode of
the bills. For Miss Nancy, the night she
arrived, had collected all the household accounts, including the highly esteemed pass-
book, — they were all of the one kind, un
paid, — and had dispatched Chad early in
the morning to the several creditors with
his pocket full of crisp bank-notes.

Chad had returned from this liquidating
tour, and the full meaning of that trusty
agent's mission had dawned upon the colonel.   He buttoned his coat tightly over his
chest, straightened himself up, sought out
his aunt, and said, with some dignity and a
slightly injured air : —

" Nancy, yo' interfe'ence in my household affairs this mornin' was vehy creditable to yo' heart, and deeply touches me ;
but if I thought you regarded it in any
other light except as a short tempo'ary
loan, it would offend me keenly. Within
a few days, however, I shall receive a vehy
large amount of secu'ities from an English
syndicate that is investigatin' my railroad.
I shall then return the amount to you with
interest, together with that other sum
which you loaned me when I left Caarter
Hall."

The little lady's only reply was to slip
her hand into his and kiss him on the forehead.

And yet that very morning he had turned
his pockets inside out for the remains of
the last dollar of the money she had given
him when he left home. When it had all
been raked together, and its pitiable insuffi-
ciency had become apparent, this dialogue
took place : —

"Chad, did you find any money on the
flo' when you breshed my clothes?"

"No, Colonel."

"Look round on the mantelpiece ; perhaps I left some bills under the clock."

"Ain't none dar, sah."

Then Chad, with that same anxious look
suddenly revived in his face, went below into
the kitchen, mounted a chair, took down
an old broken tea-cup from the top shelf,
and poured out into his wrinkled palm a
handful of small silver coin — his entire collection of tips, and all the money he had.
This he carried to the colonel, with a lie
in his mouth that the recording angel
blotted out the moment it fell from his
lips.

"Here's some change, Marsa George, I

forgot to gib ye; been left ober from de marketin'."

And the colonel gathered it all in, and went out and spent every penny of it on roses for "dear Nancy!"

All of these things, as I have said, had acted like a tonic on the colonel, bracing him up to renewed efforts, and reacting on his guests, who in return did their best to make the breakfast a merry one.

Fitz, always delightful, was more brilliant than ever, his native wit, expressed in a brogue with verbal shadings so slight that it is hardly possible to give it in print, keeping the table in a roar; while Miss Nancy, encouraged by the ease and freedom of everybody about her, forgot for a time her quiet reserve, and was charming in the way she turned over the leaves of her own youthful experiences.

And so the talk went on until, with a smile to everybody, the little lady rose, called Chad, who stood ready with shawl and cushion, and, saying she would retire to her room until the gentlemen had finished smoking, disappeared through the doorway.

The talk had evidently aroused some

memory long buried in the colonel's **mind**; for when Fitz had gone the dear old fellow picked up the glass holding the roses which he had given his aunt in the morning, and, while repeating her name softly to himself, buried his face in their fragrance. Something, perhaps, in their perfume stirred that haunting memory the deeper, for he suddenly raised his head and burst out : —

" Ah, Major, you ought to have seen that woman forty years ago ! Why, suh, she was just a rose herself ! "

And then followed in disconnected scraps, as if he were recalling it to himself, with long pauses between, that story which I had heard hinted at before. A story never told the children, and never even whispered in aunt Nancy's presence, — the one love affair of her life.

She and Robert had grown up together, — he a tall, brown-eyed young fellow just out of the university, and she a fair-haired, joyous girl with half the county at her feet. Nancy had not loved him at first, nor ever did until the day he had saved her life in that wild dash across country when her horse took fright, and he, riding neck and neck, had lifted her clear of her saddle. After

that there had been but one pair of eyes
and arms for her in the wide world. All
of that spring and summer, as the colonel
put it, she was like a bird pouring out her
soul in one continuous song. Then there
had come a night in Richmond, — the night
of the ball, — followed by her sudden return home, hollow-eyed and white, and the
mysterious postponement of the wedding
for a year.

Everybody wondered, but no one knew,
and only as the months went by did her
spirits gain a little, and she begin to sing
once more.

It was at a great party on a neighboring
estate, amid the swim of the music and the
whirl of soft lace. Suddenly loud voices
and threats, a shower of cards flung at a
man's face, an uplifted arm caught by the
host. Then a hall door thrust open and a
half-frenzied man with disordered dress
staggering out. Then the startled face of
a young girl all in white and a cry no one
ever forgot : —

"Oh, Robert! Not again?"

Her long ride home in the dead of the
night, Nancy alone in the coach, her escort
— a distant cousin — on horseback behind.

Then the pursuit. The steady rise and
fall of the hoof-beats back in the forest ; the
reining in of Robert's panting horse covered
with foam ; his command to halt ; a flash,
and then that sweet face stretched out in
the road in the moonlight by the side of
the overturned coach, the cousin bending
over her with a bullet hole in his hat, and
Robert, ghastly white and sobered, with the
smoking pistol in his hand.

Then the long, halting procession home-
ward in the gray dawn.

It was not so easy after this to keep the
secret shut away ; so one day, when the
shock had passed, — her arms about her
uncle's neck, — the whole story came out.
She told of that other night there in Richmond, with Robert reeling and half crazed ;
of his promise of reform, and the postponement of the wedding, while she waited and
trusted : so sad a story that the old uncle
forgot all the traditions that bound Southern families, and sustained her in her de-
termination never to see Robert again.

For days the broken-hearted lover haunt-
ed the place, while an out-bound ship waited
in Norfolk harbor.

Even Robert's father, crushed and hu-

miliated by it all, had made no intercession
for him. But now, he begged, would she
see his son for the last time, only that he
might touch her hand and say good-by?

That last good-by lasted an hour, Chad
walking his horse all the while before the
porch door, until that tottering figure, holding to the railings and steadying itself, came
down the steps.

A shutter thrown back, and Nancy at
the open window watching him mount.

As he wheels he raises his hat. She
pushes aside the climbing roses.

In an instant he has cleared the garden
beds, and has reined in his horse just below her window-sill. Looking up into her
face : —

" Nancy, for the last time, shall I stay?"

She only shakes her head.

" Then look, Nancy, look! This is your
work!"

A gleam of steel in a clenched hand, a
burst of smoke, and before Chad can reach
him Nancy's lover lies dead in the flowers
at her feet.

It had not been an easy story for the
colonel. When he ceased he passed his

hand across his forehead as if the air of the room stifled him. Then laying down his pipe, he bent once more over the slender vase, his face in the roses.

" May I come in ? "

In an instant the colonel's old manner returned.

" May you come in, Nancy ? Why, you dear woman, if you had stayed away five minutes longer I should have gone for you myself. What ! Another skein of yarn ? "

" Yes," she said, seating herself. " Hold out your hands."

The loop slipped so easily over the colonel's arms that it was quite evident that the rôle was not new to him.

" Befo' I forget it, Nancy, Mr. Fitzpatrick was called suddenly away to attend to some business connected with my railroad, and left his vehy kindest regards for you, and his apologies for not seein' you befo' he left."

Fitz had said nothing that resembled this, so far as my memory served me, but it was what he ought to have done, and the colonel always corrected such little slips of courtesy by supplying them himself.

"Politeness," he would sometimes say, "is becomin' rarer every day. I tell you, suh, the disease of bad manners is mo' contagious than the small-pox."

So the deception was quite pardonable in him.

"And what does Mr. Fitzpatrick think of the success of your enterprise, George?"

The colonel sailed away as usual with all his balloon topsails set, his sea-room limited only by the skein, while his aunt wound her yarn silently, and listened with a face expressive at once of deep interest and hope, mingled with a certain undefined doubt.

As the ball grew in size, she turned to me, and, with a penetration and practical insight into affairs for which I had not given her credit, began to dissect the scheme in detail. She had heard, she said, that there was lack of connecting lines and consequent absence of freight, as well as insufficient harbor facilities at Warrentown.

I parried the questions as well as I could, begging off on the plea that I was only a poor devil of a painter with a minimum knowledge of such matters, and ended by referring her to Fitz.

The colonel, much to my surprise, listened to every word without opening his lips — a silence encouraged at first by his pride that she could talk so well, and maintained thereafter because of certain misgivings awakened in his mind as to the ultimate success of his pet enterprise.

When she had punctured the last of his little balloons, he laid his hand on her shoulder, and, looking into her face, said : —

"Nancy, you really don't mean that my railroad will *never* be built ? "

"No, George ; but suppose it should not earn its expenses ? "

Her thoughts were new to the colonel. Nobody except a few foolish people in the Street, anxious to sell less valuable securities, and utterly unable to grasp the great merits of the Cartersville and Warrentown Air Line Railroad plan, had ever before advanced any such ideas in his presence. He loosened his hands from the yarn, and took a seat by the window. His aunt's misgivings had evidently so thoroughly disturbed him that for an instant I could see traces of a certain offended dignity, coupled with a nervous anxiety lest her inquiries had shaken my own confidence in his scheme.

He began at once to reassure me. There was nothing to be uneasy about. Look at the bonds! Note the perfect safety of the plan of finance — the earlier coupons omitted, the subsequent peace of the investor! The peculiar location of the road, with the ancestral estates dotted along its line! The dignity of the several stations! He could hear them now in his mind called out as they whistled down brakes: "Carter Hall! Barboursville! Talcott!" No; there was nothing about the road that should disturb his aunt. For all that a still more anxious look came into his face. He began pacing the floor, buried in deep thought, his thumbs hooked behind his back. At last he stopped and took her hand.

"Dear Nancy, if anything should happen to you it would break my heart. Don't be angry, it is only the major; but yo' talk with him has so disturbed me that I am determined to secure you against personal loss."

Miss Nancy raised her eyes wonderingly. She evidently did not catch his meaning.

"You have been good enough, my dear, to advance me certain sums of money which I still owe. I want to pay these now."

"But, George, you " —

"My dearest Nancy," — and he stooped down, and kissed her cheek, — " I will have my way. Of co'se you did n't mean anything, only I cannot let another hour pass with these accounts unsettled. Think, Nancy; it is my right. The delay affects my honor."

The little lady dropped her knitting on the floor, and looked at me in a helpless way.

The colonel opened the table drawer, and handed me pen and ink.

"Now, Major, take this sheet of paper and draw a note of hand."

I looked at his aunt inquiringly. She nodded her head in assent.

"Yes, if it pleases George."

I began with the usual form, entering the words "I promise to pay," and stopped for instructions:

"Payable when, Colonel?" I asked.

"As soon as I get the money, suh."

"But you will do that anyhow, George."

"Yes, I know, Nancy; but I want to settle it in some safe way."

Then he gazed at the ceiling in deep thought.

"I have it, Major!" And the colonel seized the pen. The note read as follows : —

On demand I promise to pay Ann Carter the sum of six hundred dollars, value received, with interest at the rate of six per cent. from January 1st.

Payable as soon as possible.

GEORGE FAIRFAX CARTER.

I looked to see what effect this unexpected influx of wealth would produce on the dear lady; but the trustful smile never wavered.

She read to the very end the modest scrap of paper so suddenly enriched by the colonel's signature, repeated in a whisper to herself "Payable as soon as possible," folded it with as much care as if it had been a Bank of England note, then thanked the colonel graciously, and tucked it in her reticule.

CHAPTER V

An Allusion to a Yellow Dog

THE colonel's office, like many other of his valued possessions, was in fact the property of somebody else.

It really belonged to a friend of Fitzpatrick, who had become so impressed by the Virginian's largeness of manner and buoyancy of enthusiasm that he had whispered to Fitz to bring him in at once and give him any desk in the place ; adding that "in a sagging market the colonel would be better than a war boom."

So the colonel moved in — not a very complicated operation in his case ; his effects being confined to an old leather portfolio and a bundle of quill pens tied up with a bit of Aunt Nancy's white yarn. The following day he had nailed his visiting card above the firm's name in the corridor, hung his hat and coat on the proprietor's peg, selected a desk nearest the light, and

was as much at home in five minutes as if
he owned the whole building.

There was no price agreed upon. Once,
when Fitz delicately suggested that all

such rents were
generally payable
monthly, the colo-
nel, after some dif-
ficulty in grasp-
ing the idea, had
said : —

"I could not of-
fer it, suh. These
gentlemen have
treated me with a
hospitality so generous that its memory
will never fade from my mind.   I cannot
bring our relations down to the level of
bargain and sale, suh ; it would be vulgar."

The colonel was perfectly sincere. As
for himself he would have put every room
in his own Carter Hall at their service for
any purpose or for any length of time, and
have slept in the woodshed himself ; and
he would as soon have demanded the value
of the bottle of wine on his own table as
ask pay for such trivial courtesies.

Nor did he stop at the rent. The free use of stamps, envelopes, paper, messenger service, and clerks were to him only evidences of a lordly sort of hospitality which endeared the real proprietor of the office all the more to him, because it recalled the lavish display of the golden days of Carter Hall.

"Permit a guest to stamp his own letters, suh? Never! Our servants attended to that."

Really he owed his host nothing. No office of its size in the Street made so much money for its customers in a bull market. Nobody lost heart in a tumble and was sold out — that is, nobody to whom the colonel talked. Once convince the enthusiastic Virginian that the scheme was feasible, — and how little eloquence was needed for that! — and the dear old fellow took hold with as much gusto as if it had been his own.

The vein in the copper mine was always going to widen out into a six-foot lead; never by any possibility could it grow any smaller. The trust shares were going up — "not a point or two at a time, gentlemen, but with the spring of a panther,

suh." Of course the railroad earnings
were a little off this month, but wait until
the spring opened; "then, suh, you will
see a revival that will sweep you off yo'
feet."

Whether it was good luck, or the good
heart that the colonel put into his friend's
customers, the results were always the
same. Singular as it may seem, his cheery
word just at the right time tided over the
critical moment many an uncertain watcher
at the "ticker," often to an enlargement
of his bank account. Nor would he allow
any one to pay him for any service of this
kind, even though he had spent days en-
grossed in their affairs.

"Take money, suh, for helpin' a friend
out of a hole? My dear suh, I see you do
not intend to be disco'teous; but look at
me, suh! There 's my hand; never refer
to it again." And then he would offer the
offender his card in the hope, perhaps, that
its ample record might furnish some further slight suggestion as to who he really
was.

His popularity, therefore, was not to be
wondered at. Everybody regarded him
kindly, total stranger as he was, and al-

though few of them believed to any extent in his "Garden Spot of Virginia," as
his pet enterprise soon came to be known
around the Street, everybody wished it well,
and not a few would have started it with a
considerable subscription could the colonel
have managed the additional thousands required to set it on its financial legs.

Fitz never lost heart in the scheme, —
that is, never when the colonel was about.
As the weeks rolled by and one combination after the other failed, and the well-
thumbed bundle of papers in the big blue
envelope was returned with various com-
ments : " In view of our present financial
engagements we are unable to undertake
your very attractive railroad scheme," or
the more curt "Not suited to our line of
customers," he would watch the colonel's
face anxiously, and rack his brain for some
additional excuse.

He always found one. Tight money, or
news from Europe, or an overissue of similar bonds ; next week it would be better.
And the colonel always believed him. Fitz
was his guiding star, and would lead him to
some safe haven yet. This faith was his
stronghold, and his only one.

This morning, however, there was a
touch of genuine enthusiasm about Fitz.
He rushed into the office, caught up the
blue bundle and the map, nearly upsetting
the colonel, who was balanced back in his
chair with his long legs over the desk, —
a favorite attitude when down town, —
rushed out, and returned in half an hour
with a fat body surmounted by a bald head
fringed about with gray curls.

He was the advance agent of that mysterious combination known to the financial
world as an " English syndicate," an elusive

sort of commercial sea-serpent with its head in London and its tail around the globe. The "inquiry" which had so gladdened the colonel's heart the morning of the breakfast with aunt Nancy had proceeded from this rotund negotiator.

The colonel had, as usual, started the road at Cartersville, and had gotten as far as the double-span iron bridge over the Tench when the rotund gentleman asked abruptly, —

"How far are you from a coal-field?"

The colonel lifted the point of his pen, adjusted his glasses, and punched a hole in the rumpled map within a hair's breadth of a black dot labeled "Cartersville."

"Right there, suh. Within a stone's throw of our locomotives."

Fitz looked into the hole with as much astonishment as if it were the open mouth of the mine itself.

"Hard or soft?" said the stout man.

"Soft, suh, and fairly good coal, I understand, although I have never used it, suh; my ancestors always burned wood."

Fitz heard the statement in undisguised wonder. In all his intercourse with the colonel he had never before known him to depart so much as a razor's edge from the truth.

The fat man communed with himself a moment, and then said suddenly, " I 'll take the papers and give you an answer in a week," and hurried away.

" Do you really mean, Colonel," said Fitz, determined to pin him down, "that there is a single pound of coal in Cartersville?"

" Do I mean it, Fitz? Don't it crop out in half a dozen spots right on our own place? One haalf of my estate, suh, is a coal-field."

" You never told me a word about it."

" I don't know that I did, Fitz. But it has never been of any use to me. Besides, suh, we have plenty of wood. We never burn coal at Caarter Hall."

Fitz did not take that view of it. He went into an exhaustive cross-examination of the colonel on the coal question: who had tested it, the character of the soil, width of the vein, and dip of the land. This information he carefully recorded in a small book which he took from his inside pocket.

Loosened from Fitz's pinioning grasp, the colonel, entirely oblivious to his friend's

sudden interest in the coal-field, and slightly impatient at the delay, bounded like a
balloon with its anchors cut.

" An answer from the syndicate within
a week! My dear Fitz, I see yo' drift.
You have kept the Garden Spots for the
foreign investors. That man is impressed,
suh; I saw it in his eye."

The room began filling up with the various customers and loungers common to
such offices : the debonair gentleman in
check trousers and silk hat, with a rose in
his button-hole, who dusts his trousers
broadside with his cane — short of one hundred shares with thirty per cent. margin ;
the shabby old man with a solemn face
who watches the ticker a moment and then
wanders aimlessly out, looking more like
an underpaid clerk in a law office than the
president of a crosstown railroad — long of
one thousand shares with no margin at all ;
the nervous man who stops the messenger
boys and devours the sales' lists before
they can be skewered on the files, — not
a dollar's interest either way ; and, last of
all, the brokers with little pads and nimble
pencils.

The news that the great English syndi-

cate was looking into the C. & W. A. L.
R. R. was soon around the office, and each
habitué had a bright word for the colonel,
congratulating him on the favorable turn
his affairs had taken.

All but old Klutchem, a broker in un-
listed securities, who had been trying for
weeks to get a Denver land scheme before
the same syndicate, and had failed.

" Garden Spot bonds ! Bosh ! Road begins nowhere and ends nowhere. If any
set of fools built it, the only freight it would
get, outside of peanuts and sweet potatoes,

would be razor-back hogs and niggers. I
would n't give a yellow dog for enough of
those securities to paper a church."

The colonel was on his feet in an instant.

"Mr. Klutchem, I cannot permit you,
suh, to use such language in my presence
unrebuked ; you " —

"Now, see here, old Garden Spot, you
know " —

The familiarity angered the colonel even
more than the outburst.

"Caarter, suh, — George Fairfax Caarter," said the colonel with dignity.

"Well, Caarter, then," mimicking him,
perhaps unconsciously. "You know " —

The intonation was the last straw. The
colonel lost all control of himself. No man
had ever thus dared before.

"Stop, Mr. Klutchem ! What I know,
suh, I decline to discuss with you. Yo'
statements are false, and yo' manner of
expressin' them quite in keepin' with the
evident vulga'ity of yo' mind. If I can as-
certain that you have ever had any claim to
be considered a gentleman you will hear
from me ag'in. If not, I shall rate you as
rankin' with yo' yallar dog ; and if you ever

speak to me ag'in I will strike you, suh, with my cane."

And the colonel, his eyes flashing, strode into the private office with the air of a field marshal, and shut the door.

Klutchem looked around the room and into the startled faces of the clerks and bystanders, burst into a loud laugh, and left the office. On reaching the street he met Fitz coming in.

"Better look after old Garden Spot, Fitzpatrick. I poked holes in his road, and he wanted to swallow me alive."

CHAPTER VI

Certain Important Letters

WHEN I reached my lodgings that night I found this note, marked in the left-hand corner "Important," and in the right-hand corner "In haste." A boy had left it half an hour before.

Be at my house at six, prepared to leave town at an hour's notice.

CARTER.

I hurried to Bedford Place, dived through the tunnel, and found Fitzpatrick with his hand on the knocker. I followed him through the narrow hall and into the dining-room. He had a duplicate, also marked "Important" and "In haste," with this additional postscript: "Bring address of a prudent doctor."

"What does all this mean, Fitz?" I asked, spreading my letter out.

"I give it up, Major. The last I saw of the colonel was at two o'clock. He was then in the private office writing. That old wind-bag Klutchem had been worrying him, I heard, and the colonel sat down on him hard. But he had forgotten all about it when I talked to him, for he was as calm as a clock. But what the devil, Major, does he want with a doctor? Chad!"

"Yes, sah!"

"Was the colonel sick this morning?"

"No, sah. Eat two b'iled eggs, and a dish ob ham half as big as yo' han'. He wa'n't sick, 'cause I yerd him singin' to hisself all fru de tunnel cl'ar out to de street."

We sat down and looked at each other. Could anybody else be sick? Perhaps aunt Nancy had been taken ill on her way home to Virginia, and the doctor was for the dear lady. But why a "prudent doctor," and why both of us to go?

Fitz paced up and down the room, and I sat by the open window, and looked out into the dreary yard. The hands of the clock in the tall tower outlined against the evening sky were past the hour, long past, and yet no colonel.

Suppose he had been suddenly stricken down himself! Suppose —

The slamming of the outer gate, followed by a sentry-like tread in the tunnel, cut short our quandary, and the colonel's tall figure emerged from the archway, and mounted the steps.

"What has happened?" we both blurted out, opening the door for him. "Who's sick? Where are we going?"

The colonel's only reply was a pressure of our hands. Then, placing his hat with great deliberation on the hall table, he drew off his gloves, waved us before him, and took his seat at the dining-room table.

Fitz and I, now thoroughly alarmed, and quite prepared for the worst, stood on each side.

The colonel dropped his hand into his inside pocket, and drew forth three letters.

"Gentlemen, you see befo' you a man on the verge of one of the great crises of his life. You heard, Fitz, of what occurred in my office this mornin'? You know how brutally I was assaulted, and how entirely without provocation on my part? I am a Caarter, suh, and a gentleman. No man can throw discredit on an enterprise bearin' my name without bein' answerable to me."

And the colonel with great dignity opened one of the letters, and read as follows : —

51 BEDFORD PLACE.
Tuesday.

P. A. KLUTCHEM.

Sir, — You took occasion this morning, in the presence of a number of my friends, to make use of certain offensive remarks reflecting upon a great commercial enterprise to which I have lent my name. This was accompanied by a familiarity as coarse as it was unwarranted. The laws of hospitality, which your own lack of good breeding violated, forbade my having you ejected from my office on the spot.

I now demand that satisfaction to which I am entitled, and I herewith inform you that I am ready at an hour's notice to meet you at any point outside the city most convenient to yourself.

Immediately upon your reply my friend Mr. T. B. Fitzpatrick will wait upon you and arrange the details. I name Major Thos. C. Yancey of Virginia as my second in the field.

I have the honor to remain

Your obedient servant,

GEORGE FAIRFAX CARTER,

Late Colonel C. S. A.

"Suffering Moses!" cried out Fitz.
"You are not going to send that?"

"It is sent, my dear Fitz. Mailed from my office this afternoon. This is a copy."

Fitz sank into a chair with both hands to his head.

"My object in sendin' for you both," the colonel continued, "was to be fully prepared should my antagonist select some early hour in the mornin'. In that case, Fitz, I shall have to rely on you alone, as Major Yancey cannot reach here until the followin' day. That was why a prudent doctor might be necessary at once."

Fitz's only reply was to thump his own head, as if the situation was too overpowering for words.

The colonel, with the same deliberation, opened the second letter. It was addressed to Judge Kerfoot, informing him of the nature of the "crisis," and notifying him of his (the colonel's) intention to appoint him sole executor of his estate should fate provide that vacancy.

The third was a telegram to Major Yancey summoning him at once "to duty on the field in an affair of honor."

"I am aware, Fitz, that some secrecy

must be preserved in an affair of this kind Nawth — quite diffe'ent from our own county, and " —

" Secrecy ! Secrecy ! With that bellowing Klutchem ? Don't you know that that idiot will have it all over the Street by nine o'clock to-morrow, unless he is ass enough to get scared, get out a warrant, and clap you into the Tombs before breakfast ? O Colonel ! How *could* you do a thing like this without letting us know ? "

The colonel never changed a muscle in his face. He was courteous, even patient with Fitz, now really alarmed over the consequences of what he considered a most stupendous piece of folly. He could not, he said, sit in judgment on other gentlemen. If Fitz felt that way, it was doubtless due to his education. As for himself, he must follow the traditions of his ancestors.

" But at all events, my friends, my dear friends," — and he extended both hands, — " we must not let this affair spoil our ap'tites. Nothing can now occur until the mornin', and we have ample time befo' daylight to make our preparations. Major, kindly touch the bell. Thank you ! Chad, serve the soup."

So short a time elapsed between the sound of the bell and the thrusting in of Chad's head that it was quite evident the darky had been listening on the outside.

If, however, that worthy guardian of the honor and dignity of the Carter family was at all disturbed by what he had heard, there was nothing in his face to indicate it. On the contrary, every wrinkle was twisted into curls and curves of hilarity. He even went so far during dinner as to correct his master in so slight a detail as to where Captain Loynes was hit in the famous duel between the colonel's father and that distinguished Virginian.

"Are you shore, Chad, it was in the leg?"

"Yès, sah, berry sho. You don't reckel-member, Colonel; but I had Marsa John's coat, an' I wrop it round Cap'in Loynes when he was ca'aied to his ca'aige. Yes, sah, jes above de knee. Marsa John picked him de fust shot."

"I remember now. Yes, you are right. The captain always walked a little lame."

"But, gentlemen," — still with great dignity, but yet with an air as if he desired to relieve our minds from any anxiety con-

cerning himself, — "by far the most interesting affair of honor of my time was the
one in which I met Major Howard, a prominent member of the Fairfax County bar.
Some words in the heat of debate led to a
blow, and the next mornin' the handkerchief was dropped at the edge of a wood
near the cote-house just as the sun rose
over the hill.   As I fired, the light blinded
me, and my ball passed through his left
arm.   I escaped with a hole in my sleeve."

"Living yet?" said Fitz, repressing a
smile.

"Certainly, suh, and one of. the fo'most
lawyers of our State.   Vehy good friend of
mine.   Saw him on'y the week befo' I left
home."

When dinner was served, I could detect
no falling off in the colonel's appetite.
With the exception of a certain nervous
expectance, intensified when there was a
rap at the front door, followed by a certain
consequent disappointment when Chad announced the return of a pair of shoes —
out to be half-soled — instead of the long-
delayed reply from the offending broker,
he was as calm and collected as ever.

It was only when he took from his table

drawer some sheets of foolscap, spread the
nib of a quill pen on his thumb nail, and
beckoned Fitz to his side, that I noticed
any difference even in his voice.

"You know, Fitz, that my hand is not so
steady as it was, and if I should fall, there
are some things that must be attended to.
Sit here and write these memoranda at my
dictation."

Fitz drew nearer, and bent his ear in
attention.

"I, George Fairfax Caarter of Caarter
Hall, Caartersville, Virginia, bein' of sound
mind " —

The pen scratched away.

"Everything down but the sound mind,"
said Fitz ; "but go on."

"Do hereby," continued the colonel.

"What 's all this for — another challenge ? " said Fitz, looking up.

"No, Fitz," — the colonel did not like
his tone, — "but a few partin' instructions
which will answer in place of a more for-
mally drawn will."

Fitz scratched on until the preamble was
finished, and the unincumbered half of Carter Hall had been bequeathed to "my ever
valued aunt Ann Carter, spinster," and he

had reached a new paragraph beginning
with, "All bonds, stocks, and shares,
whether founders', preferred, or common,
of the corporation known as the Cartersville and Warrentown Air Line Railroad,
particularly the sum of 25,000 shares of
said company subscribed for by the undersigned, I hereby bequeath," when Fitz
stopped and laid down his pen.

"You can't leave that stock. Not transferred to you yet."

"I know it, Fitz; but I have pledged my
word to take it, and so far as I am concerned, it is mine."

Fitz looked over his glasses at me, and
completed the sentence by which this also
became "the exclusive property of Ann
Carter, spinster." Then followed a clause
giving his clothes to Chad, his seal and
chain to Fitz, and his fowling-piece to me.

When the document was finished, the
colonel signed it in a bold, round hand,
and attested it by a burning puddle of red
wax into which he plunged the old family
seal. Fitz and I duly witnessed it, and
then the colonel, with the air of a man
whose mind had been suddenly relieved of
some great pressure, locked the important

document in his drawer, and handed the key to Fitz.

The change now in the colonel's manner was quite in keeping with the expression of his face. All his severe dignity, all the excess of responsibility and apparent studied calmness, were gone. He even became buoyant enough to light a pipe.

Presently he gave a little start as if suddenly remembering something until that moment overlooked, then he lighted a candle, and mounted the stairs to his bedroom. In a few minutes he returned, carrying in both hands a mysterious-looking box. This he placed with great care on the table, and proceeded to unlock with a miniature key attached to a bunch which he invariably carried in his trousers pocket.

It was a square box made of mahogany, bound at each corner with brass, and bearing in the centre of the top a lozenge-shaped silver tablet engraved with a Carter coat of arms, the letters "G. F. C." being beneath.

The colonel raised the lid and uncovered the weapons that had defended the honor of the Carter family for two generations. They were the old-fashioned single-barrel

kind, with butts like those of the pirates
in a play, and they lay in a bed of faded
red velvet surrounded by ramrods, bullet-
moulds, a green pill-box labeled "G. D. Gun
Caps," some scraps of wash leather, together with a copper powder-flask and a
spoonful of bullets.   The nipples were
protected by little patches cut from an old
kid glove.

The colonel showed with great pride a
dent on one side of the barrel where a ball
had glanced, saving some ancestor's life;
then he rang the bell for Chad, and con-
signed the case to that hilarious darky very
much as the knight of a castle would place
his trusty blade in the hands of his chief
armorer.

"Want a tech o' ile in dese baals, Colonel," said Chad, examining them critically.
"Got to keep dere moufs clean if you want
dese dogs to bark right;" and he bore
away the battery, followed by the colonel,
who went down into the kitchen to see if
the fire was hot enough to cast a few extra
bullets.

Fitz and I, being more concerned about
devising some method to prevent the consequences of the colonel's rash act than in

increasing the facilities for bloodshed, remained where we were and discussed the
possible outcome of the situation.

We had about agreed that should
Klutchem demand protection of the police,
and the colonel be hauled up for violating

the law of the State, I should go bail and
Fitz employ the lawyer, when we were
startled by a sound like the snap of a per-
cussion-cap, followed by loud talking in the
front yard.

First came a voice in a commanding
tone : " Stand where you are ! Drop yo'
hand ! "

Then Chad's " Don't shoot yit, Colonel."

Fitz and I started for the front door on
a run, threw it open, and ran against Chad
standing on the top step with his back to
the panels. Over his head he held the
stub of a candle flickering in the night
wind. This he moved up and down in obedience to certain mysterious sounds which
came rumbling out of the tunnel. Beside
him on the stone step lay the brass-cor-
nered mahogany dueling case with both
weapons gone.

The only other light visible was the
glowing eye of the tall tower.

" Where 's the colonel ? " we both asked
in a breath.

Chad kept the light aloft with one hand
like an ebony Statue of Liberty, and pointed
straight ahead into the tunnel with the
other.

"Mo' to the left," came the voice.

Chad swayed the candle towards the broken-down fence, and sent his magnified shadow scurrying up the measly wall and halfway over to the next house.

"So! Now steady."

The darky stood like the Sphinx, the light streaming atop of the tall candlestick, and then said from out one side of his mouth, "Spec' you gemmen better squat; she's gwineter bite."

Fitz peered into the tunnel, caught the gleam of a pistol held in a shadowy hand, made a clear leap, and landed out of range among the broken flower-pots. I sprang behind the hydrant, and at the same instant another cap snapped.

"Ah, gentlemen," said the voice emerging from the tunnel. "Had I been quite sure of myself I should have sent for you. I used to snuff a candle at fo'ty yards, and but that my powder is a little old I could do it ag'in."

CHAPTER VII

The Outcome of a Council of War

WHEN early the next morning, Fitz and
I arrived at the colonel's office he was
already on hand and in a state of high
nervous excitement. His coat, which, so
far as a coat might, always expressed in its
various combinations the condition of his
mind, was buttoned close up under his
chin, giving to his slender figure quite a
military air. He was pacing the floor with
measured tread; one hand thrust into his
bosom, senator fashion, the other held behind his back.

"Not a line, suh; not the scrape of a
pen. If his purpose, suh, is to ignore me
altogether, I shall horsewhip him on sight."

"Have you looked through the firm's
mail?" said Fitz, glad of the respite.

"Eve'ywhere, suh — not a scrap."

"I will hunt him up;" and Fitz hurried
down to Klutchem's office in the hope of
either intercepting the challenge or of pa-

cifying the object of the colonel's wrath, if
by any good chance the letter should have
been delayed until the morning.

In ten minutes he returned with the
mystifying news that Mr. Klutchem's letters had been sent to his apartment the
night before, and that a telegram had just
been received notifying his clerks that he
would not be down that day.

" Escaped, suh, has he?   Run like a
dog!   Like a yaller dog as he is!   Where
has he gone?"

" After a policeman, I guess," said Fitz.

The colonel stopped, and an expression
of profound contempt overspread his face.

" If the gentleman has fallen so low,
suh, that he proposes to go about with a
constable taggin' after his heels, you can
tell him, suh, that he is safe even from my
boot."

Then he shut the door of the private
office in undisguised disgust, leaving Fitz
and me on the outside.

" What are we going to do, Major?"
said Fitz, now really anxious.   " I am positive that old Klutchem has either left
town or is at this moment at police head-
quarters.   If so, the dear old fellow will

be locked up before sundown." Klutchem got that letter last night."

It was at once decided to head off the broker, Fitz keeping an eye on his office every half hour in the hope that he might turn up, and I completing the arrangements for the colonel's bail so as to forestall the possibility of his remaining in custody overnight.

Fitz spent the day in efforts to lay hands on Klutchem in order to prevent the law performing the same service for the colonel. My own arrangements were more easily completed, a friend properly possessed of sufficient real estate to make good his bond being in readiness for any emergency. One o'clock came, then three, then five; the colonel all the time keeping to the seclusion of his private office, Fitz watching for Klutchem, and I waiting in the larger office for the arrival of one of those clean-shaven, thick-set young men, in a Derby hat and sack-coat, the unexpected pair of handcuffs in his outside pocket.

The morning of the second day the situation remained still unchanged; Fitz had been unable to find Klutchem either at his office or at his lodgings, the colonel was still without any reply from his antagonist, and no young man answering to my fears had put in any appearance whatever.

The only new features were a telegram from Tom Yancey to the effect that he and Judge Kerfoot would arrive about noon, and another from the judge himself begging a postponement until they could reach the field.

Fitz read both dispatches in a corner by himself, with a face expressive of the effect these combined troubles were making upon his otherwise happy countenance. He then crumpled them up in his hand and slid them into his pocket.

Up to this time not a soul in the office except the colonel, Fitz, and I had the faintest hint of the impending tragedy, it being one of the colonel's maxims that all affairs of honor demanded absolute silence.

"If yo' enemy falls," he would say, "it is mo' co'teous to say nothin' but good of the dead; and when you cannot say that, better keep still. If he is alive let him do the talkin' — he will soon kill himself."

Fitz kept still because he felt sure if he

could get hold of Klutchem the whole
affair — either outcome powder or law —
could be prevented.

" Just as I had got the syndicate to look
into the coal land," said Fitz, "which is
the only thing the colonel 's got worth
talking about, here he goes and gets into a
first-class cast-iron scrape like this.   What
a lovely old idiot he is !   But I tell you,
Major, something has got to be done about
this shooting business right away !   Here
I have arranged for a meeting at the colonel's house on Saturday to discuss this
new coal development, and the syndicate's
agent is coming, and yet we can't for the
life of us tell whether the colonel will be
on his way home in a pine box or locked
up here for trying to murder that old wind-
bag.   It 's horrible !

"And to cap the climax,"— and he pulled
out the crumpled telegrams, — " here come
a gang of fire-eaters who will make it twice
as difficult for me to settle anything.   I
wish I could find Klutchem !"

While he spoke the office door opened,
ushering in a stout man with a red face,
accompanied by an elderly white-haired gentleman, in a butternut suit.   The red-faced

man was carrying a carpet bag — not the
Northern variety of wagon-curtain canvas,
but the old-fashioned carpet kind with
leather handles and a mouth like a catfish.
The snuff-colored gentleman's only charge
was a heavy hickory cane and an umbrella
with a waist like a market-woman's.

The red-faced man took off a wide straw
hat and uncovered a head slightly bald and
reeking with perspiration.

"I 'm lookin' fur Colonel Caarter, suh.
Is he in?"

Fitz pointed to the door of the private
office, and the elderly man drew his cane
and rapped twice. The colonel must have
recognized the signal as familiar, for the
door opened with a spring, and the next
moment he had them both by the hands.

"Why, Jedge, this is indeed an honor —
and Tom! Of co'se I knew you would
come, Tom; but the Jedge I did not expec'
until I got yo' telegram. Give me yo' bag,
and put yo' umbrella in the corner.

"Here Fitz, Major; both of you come
in here at once.

"Jedge Kerfoot, gentlemen, of the district co'te of Fairfax County. Major Tom
Yancey, of the army."

The civilities over, extra chairs were brought in, the door again closed, and a council of war was held.

Major Yancey's first word — but I must describe Yancey. Imagine a short, oily skinned, perpetually perspiring sort of man of forty, with a décolleté collar, a double-breasted waistcoat with glass buttons, and skin-tight light trousers held down to a pair of high-heeled boots by leather straps. The space between his waistband and his waistcoat was made good by certain puckerings of his shirt anxious to escape the thralldom of his suspenders. His paunch began and ended so suddenly that he constantly reminded you of a man who had swallowed a toy balloon.

Yancey's first word was an anxious inquiry as to whether he was late, adding, " I came ez soon ez I could settle some business mattahs." He had borrowed his traveling expenses from Kerfoot, who in turn had borrowed them from Miss Nancy, keeping the impending duel carefully concealed from that dear lady, and reading only such part of the colonel's letter as referred to the drawing up of some important papers in which he was to figure as chief executor.

"Late? No, Tom," said the colonel; "but the scoundrel has run to cover. We are watchin' his hole."

"You sholy don't tell me he's got away, Colonel?" replied Major Yancey.

"What could I do, Yancey? He hasn't had the decency to answer my letter."

Yancey, however, on hearing more fully the facts, clung to the hope that the Yankee would yet be smoked out.

"I of co'se am not familiar with the code as practiced Nawth — perhaps these delays are permis'ble; but in my county a challenge is a ball, and a man is killed or wounded ez soon ez the ink is dry on the papah. The time he has to live is only a mattah of muddy roads or convenience of seconds. Is there no way in which this can be fixed? I doan't like to return home without an effo't bein' made."

The colonel, anxious to place the exact situation before Major Yancey so that he might go back fully assured that everything that a Carter could do had been done, read the copy of the challenge, gave the details of Fitz's efforts to find Klutchem, the repeated visits to his office, and finally the call at his apartments.

The major listened attentively, consulted aside with the judge, and then in an authoritative tone, made the more impressive by the decided way with which he hitched up his trousers, said : —

"You have done all that a high-toned Southern gemman could do, Colonel. Yo' honor, suh, is without a stain."

In which opinion he was sustained by Kerfoot, who proved to be a ponderous sort of old - fashioned county judge, and who accentuated his decision by bringing down his cane with a bang.

While all this was going on in the private office under cover of profound secrecy, another sort of consultation of a much more public character was being held in the office outside.

A very bright young man — one of the clerks — held in his hand a large envelope, bearing on one end the printed address of the firm whose private office the colonel was at that moment occupying as a council chamber. It was addressed in the colonel's well-known round hand. This was not the fact, however, which excited interest; for the colonel never used any other envelopes than those of the firm.

The postman, who had just taken it from his bag, wanted to deliver it at its destination. The proprietor wanted to throw it back into the box for remailing, believing it to be a Garden Spot circular, and so of no especial importance. The bright young man wanted to return it to the colonel.

The bright young man prevailed, rapped at the door, and laid the letter under the colonel's nose. It bore this address : —

P. A. KLUTCHEM, ESQ.,

Room 21, Star Building, Wall Street,

Immediate. New York.

The colonel turned pale and broke the seal. Out dropped his challenge!

"Where did you get this?" he asked, aghast.

"From the carrier. It was held for postage."

Had a bombshell been exploded the effect could not have been more startling.

Yancey was the first man on his feet.

"And the scoundrel never got it! Here, Colonel, give me the letter. I'll go through

this town like a fine-tooth comb but what
I'll find him. He will never escape me.
My name is Yancey, suh!"

The judge was more conservative. He
had grave doubts as to whether a second
challenge, after a delay of two days and
two nights, could be sent at all. The traditions of the Carter family were a word
and a blow, not a blow and a word in two
days. To intrust the letter to the United
States mail was a grave mistake ; the colonel might have known that it would mis-
carry.

Fitz said grimly that letters always did,
without stamps. The Government was
running the post-office on a business basis,
not for its health.

Yancey looked at Fitz as if the interrup-
tion wearied him, then, turning to the colonel, said that he was dumbfounded that a
man who had been raised as Colonel Carter could have violated so plain a rule of
the code. A challenge should always be
delivered by the hand of the challenger's
friend. It should never be mailed.

The poor colonel, who since the discovery of the unstamped letter had sat in a
heap buried in his coat collar, — the mili-

tary button having given way, — now gave
his version of the miscarriage.

He began by saying that when his friend
Major Yancey became conversant with all
the facts he would be more lenient with
him.　He had, he said, found the proprietor's drawer locked, and, not having a stamp
about him, had dropped the document into
the mail-box with the firm's letters, pre-
suming that the clerks would affix the tax
the Government imposed.　That the document had reached the post-office was evi-
denced by the date-stamp on the envelope.
It seemed to him a picayune piece of business on the part of the authorities to detain it, and all for the paltry sum of two
cents.

Major Yancey conferred with the judge
for a moment, and then said that the colonel's explanation had relieved him of all
responsibility.　He owed him a humble
apology, and he shook his hand.　Colonel
Carter had done all that a high-bred gentleman could do.　The letter was intrusted
to the care of Mr. Klutchem's own government, the post-office as now conducted
being peculiarly a Yankee institution.

"If Mr. Klutchem's own government,

gemmen," — and he repeated it with a rising voice, — "if Mr. Klutchem's own government does not trust him enough to deliver to him a letter in advance of a payment
of two cents, such action, while highly dis-
creditable to Mr. Klutchem, certainly does
not relieve that gemman from the responsibility of answerin' Colonel Caarter."

The colonel said the point was well taken,
and the judge sustained him.

Yancey looked around with the air of a
country lawyer who had tripped up a witness, decorated a corner of the carpet, and
continued : —

"My idee, suh, now that I am on the
ground, is for me to wait upon the gemman
at once, hand him the orig'nal challenge,
and demand an immediate answer. That
is," turning to Fitz, "unless he is in hid-
in'."

Fitz replied that it was pretty clear to
him that a man could not hide from a challenge he had never received. It was quite
evident that Klutchem was detained somewhere.

The colonel coincided, and said in justice to his antagonist that he would have
to acquit him of this charge. He did not

now believe that Mr. Klutchem had run away.

Fitz, who up to this time had enjoyed every turn in the discussion, and who had listened to Yancey with a face like a stone god, his knees shaking with laughter, now threw another bombshell almost as disastrous as the first.

" Besides, gentlemen, I don't think Mr. Klutchem's remarks were insulting."

The colonel's head rose out of his collar with a jerk, and the forelegs of Yancey's chair struck the floor with a thump. Both sprang to their feet. The judge and I remained quiet. " Not insultin', suh, to call a gemman a — a — Colonel, what did the scoundrel call you?"

"It was mo' his manner," replied the colonel. "He was familiar, suh, and presumin' and offensive."

Yancey broke away again, but Fitz side-tracked him with a gesture, and asked the colonel to repeat Klutchem's exact words.

The colonel gazed at the ceiling a mo ment, and replied : —

" Mr. Klutchem said that, outside of pea nuts and sweet potatoes, all my road would git for freight would be niggers and razor-back hogs."

" Mr. Klutchem was right, Colonel," said Fitz. " Very sensible man. They will form a very large part of our freight. Anything offensive in that remark of Klutchem's, Major Yancey ? "

The major conferred with the judge, and said reluctantly that there was not.

" Go on, Colonel," continued Fitz.

" Then, suh, he said he would n't trade a yaller dog for enough of our bonds to papah a meetin'-house."

" Did he call you a yaller dog ? " said Yancey searchingly, and straightening himself up.

" No."

" Call anybody connected with you a yaller dog ? "

" Can't say that he did."

" Call yo' railroad a yaller dog ? "

" No, don't think so," said the colonel, now thoroughly confused and adrift.

Yancey consulted with the judge a moment in one corner, and then said gravely : —

" Unless some mo' direct insult is stated, Colonel, we must agree with yo' friend Mr. Fitzpatrick, and consider yo' action hasty. Now, if you had pressed the gemman, and

he had called *you* a yaller dog or a liar,
somethin' might be done. Why did n't you
press him ? "

" I did, suh. I told him his statements
were false and his manners vulgar."

" And he did not talk back ? "

" No, suh ; on'y laughed."

" Sneeringly, and in a way that sounded
like ' Yo' 're another' ? "

The colonel could not remember that it
was.

Yancey ruminated, and Fitz now took a
hand.

" On the contrary, Major Yancey, Mr.
Klutchem's laugh was a very jolly laugh ;
and, under the circumstances, a laugh very
creditable to his good nature. You are
young and impetuous, but I know my
learned friend, Judge Kerfoot, will agree
with me " — here Yancey patted his toy
balloon complacently, and the judge leaned
forward with rapt attention — " when I say
that if any apologies are in order they should
not come from Mr. Klutchem."

It was delicious to note how easily Fitz
fell into the oratorical method of his hear-
ers.

" Here is a man immersed in stocks, and

totally ignorant of the boundless resources
of your State, who limits the freight of our
road to four staples, — peanuts, hogs, sweet
potatoes, and niggers. As a further ex-
hibition of his ignorance he estimates the
value of a large block of our securities as
far below the price set upon a light, tan-
colored canine, a very inexpensive animal ;
or, as he puts it, and perhaps too coarsely,
— a yellow dog. For the expression of these
financial opinions in an open office during
business hours he is set upon, threatened
with expulsion, and finally challenged to a
mortal duel. I ask you, as chivalric Vir-
ginians, is this right ?"

Yancey was about to answer, when the
judge raised his hand impressively.

"The co'te, not being familiar with the
practice of this section, can on'y decide the
question in acco'dance with the practice of
his own county. The language used is not
objectionable, either under the law or by
the code. The prisoner, Klutchem, is dis-
charged with a reprimand, and the plain-
tiff, Caarter, leaves the co'te room without
a stain on his cha'acter. The co'te will now
take a recess."

Fitz listened with great gravity to the
decision of the learned judge, bowed to him
with the pleased deference of the winning
attorney, grasped the colonel's hand, and
congratulated him warmly on his acquittal.

Then, locking his arm through Yancey's,
he conducted that pugnacious but parched
Virginian, together with the overworked
judge, out into the street, down a flight of
stone steps, and into an underground apartment ; from which they all emerged later
with that satisfied, cheerful air peculiar to

a group of men who have slaked their thirst.

The colonel and I remained behind. He was in no mood for such frivolity.

CHAPTER VIII

A High Sense of Honor

WHILE the judge's decision had relieved the colonel of all responsibility so far as Yancey and Cartersville were concerned, — and Yancey would be Cartersville when he was back at the tavern stove, — there was one person it had not satisfied, and that was the colonel himself.

He began pacing the floor, recounting for my benefit the various courtesies he had received since he had lived at the North, — not only from the proprietors of the office, but from every one of its frequenters. And yet after all these civilities he had so far forgotten himself as to challenge a friend of his host, a very worthy gentleman, who, although a trifle brusque in his way of putting things, was still an open-hearted man. And all because he differed with him on a matter of finance.

"The mo' I think of it, Major, the mo' I am overwhelmed by my action. It was inconsiderate, suh. It was uncalled for, suh ; and I am afraid " — and here he lowered his voice — " it was ill-bred and vulgar. What could those gentlemen who stood by have thought ? They have all been so good to me, Major. I have betrayed their hospitality. I have forgotten my blood, suh. There is certainly an apology due Mr. Klutchem."

At this juncture Fitz returned, followed by Yancey, who was beaming all over, the judge bringing up the rear.

All three listened attentively.

"Who 's goin' to apologize ?" said Yancey, shifting his thumbs from his armholes to the side pockets of his vest, from which he pinched up some shreds of tobacco.

"I am, suh !" replied the colonel.

"What for, Colonel ?" The doctrine was new to Yancey.

"For my own sense of honor, suh !"

"But he never got the challenge."

"That makes no diff'ence, suh. I wrote it." And the colonel threw his head up, and looked Major Yancey straight in the eye.

"But, Colonel, we 've got the letter. Klutchem don't know a word about it."

"But I do, Major Yancey; and so do you and Fitz, and the jedge and the major here. We all know it. Do you suppose, suh, for one instant, that I am cowardly enough to stab a man in the back this way and give him no chance of defendin' himself? It is monst'ous, suh! Why, suh, it's no better than insultin' a deaf man, and then tryin' to escape because he did not hear you. I tell you, suh, I shall apologize. Fitz, kindly inquire outside if there is any news of Mr. Klutchem."

Fitz opened the door, and sent the inquiry ringing through the office.

"Yes!" came a voice from around the "ticker." "Went to the races two days ago, got soaking wet, and has been laid up ever since at a friend's house with the worst attack of gout he ever had in his life."

The colonel started as if he had been stung, put on his hat, and with a determined air buttoned his coat over his chest. Then, charging Yancey and the judge not to leave the office until he returned, he beckoned Fitz to him, and said: —

"We have not a moment to lose. Get Mr. Klutchem's address, and order a caarriage."

It was the custom with Fitz never to
cross the colonel in any one of his sudden
whims. Whether this was because he liked
to indulge him, or because it gave him an
opportunity to study a type of man entirely
new to him, the result was always the same,
— the colonel had his way. Had the Virginian insisted upon waiting on the offending broker in a palanquin or upon the top
of a four-in-hand, Fitz would have found the
vehicle somehow, and have crawled in or
on top beside him with as much compla-
cency as if he had spent his whole life with
palanquins and coaches, and had had no
other interests. So when the order came
for the carriage, Fitz winked at me with
his left eye, walked to the sidewalk, whistled to a string of cabs, and the next instant we were all three whirling up the
crowded street in search of the bedridden
broker.

The longer the colonel brooded over the
situation the more he was satisfied with
the idea of the apology. Indeed, before
he had turned down the side street leading
to the temporary hospital of the suffering
man, he had arranged in his mind just
where the ceremony would take place, and

just how he would frame his opening sentence. He was glad, too, that Klutchem
had been discovered so soon — while Yancey and Kerfoot were still in town.

The colonel alighted first, ran up the
steps, pulled the bell with the air of a doctor called to an important case, and sent
his card to the first floor back.

"Mr. Klutchem says, 'Walk up,'" said
the maid.

The broker was in an armchair with his
back to the door, only the top of his bald
head being visible as we entered. On a
stool in front rested a foot of enormous
size swathed in bandages. Leaning against
his chair were a pair of crutches. He was
somewhat startled at the invasion, made as
it was in the busiest part of the day.

"What 's up? Anybody busted?"

Fitz assured him that the Street was in
a mood of the greatest tranquillity; that
the visit was purely personal, and made for
the express purpose of offering Colonel
Carter an opportunity of relieving his mind
of a pressure which at the precise moment
was greater than he could bear.

"Out with it, old Garden — Colonel,"
broke out Klutchem, catching himself in

time, and apparently greatly relieved that
the situation was no worse.

The colonel, who remained standing,
bowed courteously, drew himself up with a
dress-parade gesture, and recounted slowly
and succinctly the incidents of the preceding three days.

When he arrived at the drawing-up of
the challenge, Klutchem looked around
curiously, gathered in his crutches with his
well leg, — prepared for escape or defense,
— and remained thus equipped until the
colonel reached the secret consultation in
the private office and the return of the unstamped letter. Then he toppled his sup-
ports over on the floor, and laughed until
the pain in his elephantine foot bent him
double.

The colonel paused until Klutchem had
recovered himself, and then continued, his
face still serene, and still expressive of a
purpose so lofty that it excluded every
other emotion.

"The return of my challenge unopened,
suh, coupled with the broad views of my
distinguished friends Mr. Fitzpatrick and
the major, — both personal friends of yo'
own, I believe, — and the calmer reflection

of my own mind, have convinced me, Mr. Klutchem, that I have been hasty and have done you a wrong; and, suh, rememberin' my blood, I have left the cares of my office for a brief moment to call upon you at once, and tell you so. I regret, suh, that you have not the use of both yo' legs, but I have anticipated that difficulty. My caarriage is outside."

"Don't mention it, Colonel. You never grazed me. If you want to plaster that syndicate all over with Garden Spots, go ahead. I won't say a word. There's my hand."

The colonel never altered a line in his face nor moved a muscle of his body. Mr. Klutchem's hand remained suspended in mid air.

"Yo' action is creditable to yo' heart, suh, but you know, of course, that I cannot take yo' hand here. I insulted you in a public office, and in the presence of yo' friends and of mine, some of whom are at this moment awaitin' our return. I feel assured, suh, that under the circumstances you will make an effort, however painful it may be to you, to relieve me from this stain on my cha'acter. Allow me to offer you

my arm, and help you to my caarriage, suh.
I will not detain you mo' than an hour."

Klutchem looked at him in perfect astonishment.

"What for?"

The colonel's color rose.

"That this matter may be settled properly, suh.   I insulted you publicly in my
office.   I wish to apologize in the same
way.   It is my right, suh."

"But I can't walk.   Look at that foot,
— big as a hatbox."

"My friends will assist you, suh.   I will

carry yo' crutches myself. Consider my situation. You surely, as a man of honor, will not refuse me this, Mr. Klutchem?"

The colonel's eyes began to snap, and Fitz edged round to pour oil when the wind freshened. Klutchem's temper was also on the move.

"Get out of this chair with that mush poultice," pointing to his foot, "and have you cart me down to Wall Street to tell me you are sorry you did n't murder me! What do you take me for?"

The colonel's eyes now fairly blazed, and his voice trembled with suppressed anger.

"I did take you, suh, for a gentleman. I find I am mistaken. And you refuse to go, and" —

"Yes!" roared Klutchem, his voice splitting the air like a tomahawk.

"Then, suh, let me tell you right here that if you do not get up now and get into my caarriage, whenever you *can* stand on yo' wuthless legs, I will thresh you so, suh, that you will never get up any mo'."

CHAPTER IX

A Visit of Ceremony

THE Honorable I. B. Kerfoot, presiding
judge of the district court of Fairfax County, Virginia, and the gallant Major Thomas
C. Yancey, late of the Confederate army,
had been the colonel's guests at his hospitable house in Bedford Place for a period

of six days and six nights, when my cards
— two — were given to Chad, together with
my verbal hopes that both gentlemen were
within.

My visit was made in conformity with
one of the colonel's inflexible rules, — every
guest under his roof, within one week of
his arrival, was to be honored by a personal
call from every friend within reach.

No excuse would have sufficed on the
ground of flying visits. And indeed, so far
as these particular birds of passage were
concerned, the occupation was permanent,
the judge having taken possession of the
only shake-down sofa on the lower floor,
and the warlike major having plumped himself into the middle of the colonel's own bed
not ten minutes after his arrival. Even to
the casual Northern eye, unaccustomed to
the prolonged sedentary life of the average
Virginian when a guest, there was every
indication that these had come to stay.

Chad laid both of my cards on the table,
and indulged in a pantomime more graphic
than spoken word. He shut his eyes, laid
his cheek on one hand, and gave a groan of
intense disgust, followed by certain gleeful
chuckles, made the more expressive by the

sly jerking of his thumb towards the dining-room door and the bobbing up and down
of his fore-finger in the direction of the
bedroom above.

"Bofe in. Yes, sah! Bofe in, an' bofe
abed. Last I yeard from em' dey was hol-
lerin' for juleps."

I entered the dining-room and stopped
short. On a low sofa at the far end of the
room lay a man of more than ordinary
girth, with coat, vest, and shoes off, his face
concealed by a newspaper. From beneath
this sheet came, at regular intervals, a long-
drawn sound like the subdued puff of a tired
locomotive at rest on a side-track. Beside
him was an empty tumbler, decorated with
a broken straw and a spray of withered
mint.

The summer air fanned through the
closed blinds of the darkened room, and
played with the silvery locks that straggled
over the white pillow ; the paper rose and
fell with a crinkling noise, keeping time to
the rhythm of the exhaust. Beyond this
there was no movement. The Hon. I. B.
Kerfoot was asleep.

I watched the slowly heaving figure for
a moment, picked up a chair, and gently

closed the door. I could now look the colonel in the face so far as the judge was concerned. My account with the colonel was settled.

Retiring to the yard outside, which was cool and shady, and, despite its dilapidated appearance, a grateful relief from the glare of the street, I tilted my chair against the dissipated wall, with its damaged complexion of scaling white-wash, and sat down to await the colonel's return.

Meanwhile Chad busied himself about the kitchen, moving in and out the basement door, and at last brought up a great tin pan, seated himself on the lower step, and proceeded to shell pease, indulging all the while in a running commentary on the events of the preceding week.

One charm in Chad's conversation was its clearness. You always absorbed his meaning. Another was its reliability. When he finished you had the situation in full.

First came the duel.

"So dat Ketchem man done got away? Doan' dat beat all! An' de colonel a-makin' his will an' a-rubbin' up his old barkers. Can't have no fun yer naaway; sumpin'

allers spiles it.   But yer oughter seen de
colonel dat day w'en he come home ! Sakes
alive, warn't he b'ilin' ! Much as Jedge
Keerfoot could do to keep him from killin'
dat Yankee on de street."

Chad's long brown fingers fumbled
among the green pea-shells, which he
heaped up on one side of the pan, and the
conversation soon changed to his master's
" second in the field."   I encouraged this
divergence, for I had been charged by Fitz
to find out when these two recent additions
to the household in Bedford Place intended
returning to their native clime ; that loyal
friend of the colonel being somewhat disturbed over their preparations for what
promised to be a lengthy stay.

"'Fo' de Lawd, I doan' know! Tom
Yancey nebber go s' long as de mint patch
hol' out, an' de colonel bought putty near a
ba'el ob it dis mawnin', an' anudder dimi-
john from Mister Grocerman.   Makes my
blood bile to see dese Yanceys, anyhow.
See dat carpet bag w'at he fotch wid him ?
Knowed w'at he had in it w'en he opened
its mouf an' de jedge tuk his own clo'es
outen it ? A pair ob carpet slippers, two
collars, an' a lot ob chicken fixin's.   Not a

shirt to his back 'cept de one he had on! Had to stay abed yisteddy till I i'oned it. Dar's one ob his collars on de line now. Dese yer Yanceys no 'count no way. Beats de lan' how de colonel can put up wid 'em, 'cept his faader was quality. You know de old gineral married twice, de las' time his oberseer's daughter. Dat's her chile — Tom Yancey — 'sleep now on de colonel's bed upstairs wid a straw in his mouf like a shote. But de colonel say 't ain't Tom's fault dat he takes after his mammy; he's a Yancey, anyhow. But I tell you, Major, Miss Nancy doan' hab nuffin' much to do wid 'im, — she can't abide 'im."

"How long are they going to stay, Chad?" I asked, wishing to make a definite report to Fitz.

"Doan' know. Ole groun'-hog mighty comf'ble in de hole." And he heaped up another pile of shells.

"Fust night de jedge come he tol' de colonel dat Miss Nancy say we all got to come home when de month's up, railroad or no railroad. Dat was a week ago. Den de jedge tasted dat Madary Mister Grocerman sent, an' I ain't yerd nuffin' 'bout goin' home since. Is you yerd, Major?"

Before I could answer, a shutter opened overhead and a voice came sifting down.

"O Chad! Mix me a julep. And, Chad, bring an extra one for the colonel. I reckon he'll be yer d'reckly."

"Yes, sah," replied Chad, without lifting his eyes from the pan.

Then glancing up and finding the blind closed again, he said to me in a half-whisper : —

"Colonel get his julep when he ax fur it. I ain't caayin' no double drinks to nobody. Dis ain't no camp-meetin' bar."

But Chad's training had been too thorough to permit of his refusing sustenance or attention to any guest of his master's, no matter how unworthy, and it was not many minutes before he was picking over "de ba'el" containing that peculiar pungent variety of plant so common to the grave-yards of Virginia.

Before the cooling beverage had been surmounted by its delicate mouthpiece the street gate opened and the colonel walked briskly in.

"Ah, Major! You here? Jes the vehy man we wanted, suh! Fitz and the English agent are comin' to dinner. You have

heard the news, of co'se? No? Not about
the great syndicate absorbin' the Garden
Spots? My dear suh, she's floated! The
C. & W. A. L. R. R. is afloat, suh! Proudly
ridin' the waves of prosperity, suh. Wafted
on by the breeze of success."

"What, bought the bonds?" I said,
jumping up.

"Well, not exactly bought them out-
right, for these gigantic operations are not
conducted in that way ; but next to it, suh.
To-day," — and he brought his hand down
softly on my shoulder, — "to-day, suh, they
have cabled their agent — the same gentleman, suh, you saw in my office some time
ago — to make a searchin' investigation
into the mineral and agricultural resources
of that section of my State, with a view to
extendin' its railroad system. I quote, suh,
the exact words : 'extendin' its railroad system.' Think, my dear Major, of the effect
that a colossal financial concern like the
great British syndicate would produce upon
Fairfax County, backed as it is, suh, by
untold millions of stagnant capital absolutely rottin' in English banks! The road
is built!" And the colonel in his excitement opened his waistcoat, and began

pacing the yard, fanning himself vigorously
with his hat.

Chad substituted a palm-leaf fan from
the hall table, and, producing a small tray,
picked up the frosted tumbler and mounted
the three steps to relieve the thirsty guest
on the floor above.

As he reached the last step a hand
stretched out, and a voice said : —

"Jes what I wanted."

"Dis julep, Jedge, is Major Yancey's."

"All the better." And nodding to the
colonel and bowing gravely to me, the
Hon. I. B. Kerfoot settled himself on the
top of the front steps with very much the
same air with which he would have occupied his own judicial bench.

With the exception that this julep was
just begun and the other just ended, his-
Honor presented precisely the same outward appearance as when I discovered him
asleep on the sofa.

His was, in fact, the extremest limit of
dishabille permissible even on the hottest
of summer afternoons in the most retired
of back yards, — no coat, no vest, no shoes.
In one hand he held a crumpled collar and
a high, black silk stock ; with the other he

grasped the julep. His hair was tousled, his face shriveled up and pinched by his heavy nap, his eyes watery and vague. He reminded me of the man one sometimes meets in the aisle of a sleeping-car when one boards the train at a way station in the night.

" I hope you have had a refreshin' sleep, Jedge," said the colonel. " My friend the major here did himself and me the honor of callin' upon you, but findin' that you were restin', suh, he sought the cool of my co'teyard until you should awake."

His Honor looked at me over the edge of his tumbler and bowed feebly. The straw remained glued to his mouth.

"I have been tellin' him, suh, of the extr'o'd'nary boom to-day in Garden Spots, as some of my young friends call the secu-'ities of my new road, work upon which will be begun next week."

The announcement made no impression upon the judge, his face remaining sleepily stolid until that peculiar gurgling sound, the death-rattle of a dying julep, caused a shade of sadness to pass over it.

At that instant the shutter again opened overhead.

"Hello, Colonel! Home, are you?
Chad, where's my julep? Ah, Major, hope
I see you vehy well, suh. Where's Ker-
foot?"

That legal luminary craned his head forward as far as it would go without neces-
sitating any additional movement of his
body, caught Yancey's eye as he leaned
out of the window, and held up the empty
glass.

When everybody had stopped laughing
the colonel made a critical but silent exam-
ination of the judge, called to Yancey, and
said : —

"Gentlemen, we do not dine until seven.
You will both have ample time to dress."

CHAPTER X

Chad in Search of a Coal-Field

THE colonel was the first man down-
stairs. When he entered I saw at a glance
that it was one of his gala nights, for he
wore the ceremonial white waistcoat and
cravat, and had thrown the accommodating
coat wide open. His hair, too, was brushed
back from his broad forehead with more
than usual care, each silver thread keeping its proper place in the general scheme
of iron-gray ; while his goatee was twisted
to so fine a point that it curled upward
like a fishhook. He had also changed his
shoes, his white stockings now being incased in low prunellas tied with a fresh
ribbon, which hung over the toes like the
drooping ears of a lapdog.

The attention which the colonel paid to
these particular details was due, as he fre-
quently said, to his belief that a man would
always be well dressed who looked after
his extremities.

"I can inva'iably, suh, detect the gentleman under the shabbiest suit of clothes, if his collar and stockings are clean. When, besides this, he brushes his hat and blacks his shoes, you may safely invite him to dinner."

Something like this was evidently passing in his mind as he stood waiting for his guests, his back to the empty grate; for he examined his hands critically, glanced at his shoes, and then excusing himself, turned his face, and taking a pair of scissors from his pocket proceeded leisurely to trim his cuffs.

"These duties of the dressin'-room, my dear Major, should have been attended to in their proper place; but the fact is the jedge is makin' rather an elaborate toilet in honor of our guest, and as Yancey occupies my bedroom, and the jedge is also dressin' there, my own accommodations are limited. I feel sure you will excuse me."

While he spoke the door opened, and his Honor entered in a William Penn style of make-up, ruffled shirt and all. He really was not unlike that distinguished peace-maker, especially when he carried one of the colonel's long pipes in his mouth. He had, I am happy to say, since leaving the front steps, accumulated an increased amount of clothing. The upper half of the familiar butternut suit — the coat — still clung to him, but the middle and lower half had been supplanted by another waistcoat and trousers of faded nankeen, the first corrugated into wrinkles and the second flapping about his ankles.

The colonel absorbed him at a glance, and with a satisfied air placed a chair for him near the window and handed him a palm-leaf fan.

Last of all came Yancey in a flaming red necktie, the only new addition to his costume — a part, no doubt, of the "chicken fixin's" found by Chad in the carpet bag.

The breezy ex-major, as he entered, seized my hand with the warmth of a life-long friend ; then moving over and encircling with his arm the colonel's coat collar, he lowered his voice to a confidential whisper and inquired about the market of the day with as much solicitude as though his last million had been filched from him on insufficient security.

When, a few minutes later, the round-faced man, the agent of the great English syndicate, walked in, preceded by Fitz, nothing could have been more courtly than the way the colonel presented him to his guests — pausing at every name to recount some slight biographical detail complimentary to each, and ending by announcing with great dignity that his honored guest was none other than the very confidential agent and adviser of a group of moneyed magnates whose influence extended to the uttermost parts of the earth.

The agent, like many other sensible Englishmen, was a bluff, hearty sort of man, with a keen eye for the practical side of life and an equally keen enjoyment of every other, and it was not five minutes before he had located in his round head the precise standing and qualifications of every man in the room.

While Yancey amused him greatly as a type quite new to him, the colonel filled him with delight. "So frank, so courteous, so hospitable ; quite the air of a country squire of the old school," he told Fitz afterward.

As a host that night, the colonel was in

his happiest vein, and by the time the
coffee was served, had succeeded not only
in entertaining the table in his own inim-
itable way, but he had drawn out from
each one of his guests, not excepting the
reticent Fitz, some anecdote or incident
of his life, bringing into stronger relief the
finer qualities of him who told it.

Kerfoot in a ponderous way gave the
details of a murder case, tried before him
many years ago, in which the judge's
charge so influenced the jury that the man
was acquitted, and justly so, as was afterward proved. Yancey related an incident
of the war, where he, only a drummer boy
at the time, assisted, at great risk, in carrying a wounded comrade from the field.
And Fitz was forced to admit that one of
the largest financial operations of the
day would have been a failure had he not ,
stepped in at the critical moment and
saved it.

Up to this point in the dinner not the
slightest reference had been made to the
railroad or its interests except by the impetuous Yancey, who asked Fitz what the
bonds would probably be worth, and who
was promptly silenced by the colonel with

the suggestive remark that none were for
sale, especially at this time.

When, however, by the direction of the
colonel, the cloth was removed and the old
mahogany table that Chad rubbed down
every morning with a cork was left with
only the glasses, a pair of coasters and
their decanters, — the Madeira within reach
of the judge's hand, — the colonel rose
from his chair and spread out on the polished surface a stained and ragged map,
labeled in one corner in quaint letters,
" Lands of John Carter, Esquire, of Carter
Hall." Only then was the colonel ready
for business.

" This is the correct survey, I believe,
Jedge," said the colonel.

The judge emptied his glass, felt all over
his person for his spectacles, found them
in the inside pocket of his nankeen waistcoat, and, perching them on the extreme
end of his nose, looked over their rims and
remarked that the original deeds of the
colonel's estate had been based upon this
map, and that, so far as he knew, it was
correct. Then he added : —

" The partition line that was made im-
mejitly aafter the war, dividin' the estate

between Miss Ann Caarter and yo'self, Colonel, was also tuk from this survey."

Fitz conferred with the agent for a moment and then asked the colonel where lay the deposit of coal of which he had spoken.

"In a moment, my dear Fitz," said the colonel, deprecatingly, and turning to the agent : —

"The city of Fairfax, suh, that we discussed this mornin', will be located to the right of this section ; the Tench runs here ; the iron bridge, suh, should cross at this point," marking it with his thumb nail. "Or perhaps you gentlemen will decide to have it nearer the Hall. It is immaterial to me."

Then looking at Fitz : "I can't locate the coal, my dear Fitz ; but I think it is up here on the hill at the foot of the range."

The agent lost interest immediately in the iron bridge over the Tench, and asked a variety of questions about the deposit, all of which the colonel answered courteously and patiently, but evidently with a desire to change the subject as soon as possible.

The Englishman, however, was persistent, while the judge's last sententious remark regarding the recent subdivision of the estate awakened a new interest in Fitz.

What if this coal should not be on the colonel's land at all! He caught his breath at the thought.

It was Fitz's only chance to restore the colonel's fortunes; and although for obvious reasons he dared not tell him so, it was really the only interest the Englishman had in the scheme at all.

Indeed, the agent had frankly said so to Fitz, adding that he was anxious to locate a deposit of coal somewhere in the vicinity of the line of the colonel's proposed road; because the extension of certain railroads in which the syndicate was interested — not the C. & W. A. L. R. R., however — depended almost entirely upon the purchase of this vital commodity.

Full of these instructions the agent, after listening to a panegyric upon the resources of Fairfax County, interrupted rather curtly a glowing statement of the colonel's concerning the enormous value of the Garden Spot securities by asking this question : —

"Are the coal lands for sale?"

Fitz shivered at its directness, fearing that the colonel would catch the drift affairs were taking and become alarmed. His fears were groundless; the shot had gone over his head.

"No, suh! My purpose is to use it to supply our shops and motive power."

"If you should decide to sell the lands I would make an investigation at once," replied the agent, quietly, but with meaning in his voice.

The colonel looked at him eagerly.

"Would you at the same time consider the purchase of our securities?"

"I might."

"When would you go?"

"To-morrow night, or not at all. I return to England in a week."

Yancey and the judge looked at each other inquiringly with a certain anxious expression suggestive of some impending trouble. The judge recovered himself first, and quickly filled his glass, leaving but one more measure in the decanter. This measure Yancey immediately emptied into his own person, as perhaps the only place where it would be entirely safe from the treacherous thirst of the judge.

Fitz read in their faces these mental processes, and was more determined than ever to break up at once what he called " the settlement."

" Are you sho', Colonel," inquired Kerfoot, catching at straws, " that the coal lands lie entirely on yo' father's property? Does not the Barbour lan' jine yo's on the hill ? "

" I am not positively sho', suh, but I have always understood that what we call the coal hills belonged to my father. You see," said the colonel, turning to the agent, "this grade of wild lan' is never considered of much value with us, and a few hundred acres mo' or less is never insisted on among old families of our standin' whose estates jine."

Yancey expanded his vest, and said authoritatively that he was quite sure the coal hills were on the Barbour property. He had shot partridges over that land many a time.

The agent, who had listened calmly to the discussion, remarked dryly that until the colonel definitely ascertained whether he had any lands to sell it would be a useless waste of time to make the trip.

"Quite so," said Kerfoot, raising the emptied decanter to his eye, and replacing it again with a look at Yancey expressive of the contempt in which he held a man who could commit so mean an act.

"But, Colonel," said Fitz, "can't you telegraph to-morrow and find out?"

"To whom, my dear Fitz? It would take a week to get the clerk of the co'te to look through the records. Nobody at Barbour's knows."

"Does Miss Nancy know?"

The colonel shook his head dubiously.

Fitz's face suddenly lighted up as he started from his seat, and caught the colonel by the arm.

"Does Chad?"

"Chad! Yes, Chad might."

Fitz nearly overturned his chair in his eagerness to reach the top of the kitchen stairs.

"Come up here, Chad, quick as your legs can carry you — two steps at a time!"

Chad hurried into the room with the face of a man sent for to put out a fire.

"Chad," said the colonel, "you know the big hill as you go up from the marsh at home?"

"Yes, sah."

"Whose lan' is the coal on, mine or Jedge Barbour's?"

The old darky's face changed from an expression of the deepest anxiety to an effort at the deepest thought. The change was so sudden that the wrinkles got tangled up in the attempt, resulting in an expression of vague uncertainty.

"You mean, Colonel, de hill whar we cotch de big coon?"

"Yes," said the colonel encouragingly, ignorant of the coon, but knowing that there was only one hill.

"Well, Jedge Barbour's niggers always said dat de coon was dere coon, 'ca'se he was treed on dere lan', and we 'sputed dat it was our coon, 'ca'se it was on our lan'."

"Who got de coon?" asked Fitz.

"Oh, *we* got the coon!" And Chad's eyes twinkled.

"That settles it. It's your land, Colonel," said Fitz, with one of his sudden roars, in which everybody joined but Chad and the judge.

"But den, gemmen," — Chad was a little uncomfortable at the merriment, — "it was our coon for sho. I knowed whar de line

went, 'ca'se I he'p Marsa John caarry de
spy-glass when he sold de woodlan's to
Jedge Barbour, an' de coon was on our side
ob dat line."

If Chad's first statement caused nothing
but laughter, the second produced nothing
but the profoundest interest.

Here was the surveyor himself!

The colonel turned the map to Chad's
side of the table. Every man in the room
stood up and craned his head forward.

"Now, Chad," said the colonel, "this
map is a plan of our lan' — same as if you
were lookin' down on it. Here is the road
to Caartersville. See that square, black
mark? That 's Caarter Hall. This is the
marsh, and that is the coal hill. Now,
standin' here in the marsh, — this is where
our line begins, Fitz, — standin' here, Chad,
in the marsh, which side of the line is that
hill on? Mine or Jedge Barbour's?"

The old man bent over the table, and
scanned the plan closely.

"W'at 's dis blue wiggle lookin' like a
big fish-wum?"

"That 's the Tench River."

Chad continued his search, his wrinkled
brown hand, with its extended forefinger

capped by its stumpy nail, looking for all the world like a mud turtle with head out crawling over the crumpled surface of the map.

" Scuse me till I run down to de kitchen an' git my spec's.   I can't see like " —

" Here, take mine ! " said Fitz, handing him his gold ones. He would have lent him his eyes if he could have found that coal-field the sooner.

The turtle crawled slowly up, its head thrust out inquiringly, inched along the margin of the map, and backed carefully down again, pausing for such running commentaries as " Dis yer 's de ribber ; " " Dat 's de road ; " " Dis de ma'sh."

The group was now a compact mass, every eye watching Chad's finger as though it were a divining rod — Fitz full of smothered fears lest after all the prize should slip from his grasp ; the agent anxious but reserved ; Yancey and the judge hovering between hope and despair, with eyes on the empty decanter ; and last of all the colonel, on the outside, holding a candle himself, so that his guests might see the better — the least interested man in the room.

Presently the finger stopped, and Chad looked up into his master's face.

"If I was down dar, Marsa George, jes a minute, I could tole ye, 'ca'se I reckel-member de berry tree whar Marsa John had de spyglass sot on its legs. I held de pole on de rock way up yander on de hill, an' in dat berry rock Marsa John done cut a crotch."

"And which way is the crotch in the rock from the marsh here?" asked Fitz eagerly.

Chad stood up, looked at the plan glis-tening under the candlelight, paused an instant, then took off the gold-rimmed glasses, and handed them with great defer-ence to Fitz.

"'T ain't no use, Marsa George. I kin go frough dat ma'sh blindfolded in de night an' cotch a possum airy time along airy one ob dem fences ; but dis yer foolin' wid lan's · on paper is too much for Chad. 'Fo' Gawd, I doan' know !"

CHAPTER XI

Chad on his own Cabin Floor

THE night after the eventful dinner in
Bedford Place, the colonel, accompanied
by his guests, had alighted at a dreary way
station, crawled into a lumbering country
stage, and with Chad on the box as pilot,
had stopped before a great house with
ghostly trailing vines and tall chimneys
outlined against the sky.

When I left my room on the following
morning the sunlight was pouring through
the big colonial window, and the breath of
. the delicious day, laden with the sweet
smell of bending blossoms, floated in
through the open blinds.

Descending the great spiral staircase
with its slender mahogany balusters, —
here and there a break, — I caught sight
of the entrance hall below with its hanging
glass lantern, quaint haircloth sofas lining
the white walls, and half-oval tables heaped
with flowers, and so on through the wide-

open door leading out upon a vine-covered
porch. This had high pillars and low railings against which stood some broad settles — all white.

The colonel, Fitz, and the English agent
were still in their rooms, — three pairs of
polished shoes outside their several doors
bearing silent witness to the fact, — and

the only person stirring was a pleasant-
faced negro woman with white apron and
gay-colored bandana, who was polishing the
parlor floor with a long brush, her little

pickaninny astraddle on the broom end for weight.

I pushed aside the hanging vines, sat down on one of the wooden benches, and looked about me.   This, then, was Carter Hall!

The house itself bore evidence of having once been a stately home.   It was of plaster stucco, yellow washed, peeled and broken in places, with large dormer windows and sloping roof, one end of which was smothered in a tangle of Virginia creeper and trumpet vine climbing to the very chimney-top.

In front there stretched away what had once been a well-kept lawn, now a wild of coarse grass broken only by the curving line of the driveway and bordered by a row of Lombardy poplars with here and there a gap, — bitten out by hungry camp-fires.

To the right rose a line of hills increasing in height as they melted into the morning haze, and to the left lay an old-fashioned garden, — one great sweep of bloom. With the wind over it, and blowing your way, you were steeped in roses.

I began unconsciously to recall to myself all the traditions of this once famous **house.**

Yes, there must be the window where Nancy waved good-by to her lover, and there were the flower-beds into which he had fallen headlong from his horse, — only a desolate corner now with the grass and tall weeds grown quite up to the scaling wall, and the wooden shutters tightly closed. I wondered whether they had ever been opened since.

And there under my eyes stood the very step where Chad had helped his old master from his horse the day his sweetheart Henny had been purchased from Judge Barbour, and close to the garden gate were the negro quarters where they had begun their housekeeping. I thought I knew the very cabin.

And that line of silver glistening in the morning light must be the river Tench, and the bend near the willows the spot where the colonel would build the iron bridge with the double span, and across and beyond on the plateau, backed by the hills, the site of the future city of Fairfax.

I left my seat, strolled out into the garden, crossed the grass jeweled with dew, and filled my lungs with the odor of the sweet box bordering the beds, — a rare de-

light in these days of modern gardens. Suddenly I came upon a wide straw hat and a
broad back bending among the bushes. It
was Chad.

"Mawnin', Major ; fust fox out de hole,
is yer? Lawd a massey, ain't I glad ter git
back to my ole mist'ess! Lan' sakes alive!
I ain't slep' none all night a-thinkin' ober
it. You ain't seen my Henny? Dat was
her sister's chile rubbin' down de flo'. She
come ober dis mawnin' ter help, so many
folks here. Wait till I git a basket ob dese
yer ole pink rose-water roses. See how I
snip 'em short? Know what I 'm gwineter
do wid 'em? Sprinkle 'em all ober de
tablecloth. I lay dey ain't nobody done
dat for my mist'ess since I been gone.
But, Major," — here Chad laid down the
basket on the garden walk and looked at
me with a serious air, — "I done got dat
coal lan' business down to a fine p'int. I
was up dis mawnin' 'fo' daylight, an' I foun'
dat rock, an' de crotch is dar yit ; I scrape
de moss offen it myself ; an' I foun' de tree
too. I ain't sayin' nuffin', but jes you wait
till after breakfas' an' dey all go out lookin'
for de coal! Jes you wait, dat 's all! Chad 's
on his own cabin flo' now. Can't fool dis
chile no mo'."

This was good news so far as it went.
Our sudden exodus from Bedford Place had
been determined upon immediately after
Chad's dismal failure to locate the coal-field:
Fitz having carried the day against Yancey,
Kerfoot, and even the agent himself, who
was beginning to waver under the accumu-
lation of uncertainties.

"Dat's enough roses to bury up de
dishes. Rub yo' nose down in 'em. Ain't
dey sweet! Now, come along wid me,
Major. I done tole Henny 'bout you an' de
tar'pins an' de times de gemmen had. Dis
way, Major; won't take a minute, an' ef
ye all go back to-night, — an' I yerd Mister Englishman say *he* got to go, — you
might n't hab anudder chance. Henny's
cookin', ye know. Dis way. Step under
dat honeysuckle!"

I looked through an open door and into
a dingy, smoke-dried interior, ceiled with
heavy rafters, and hung with herbs, red
peppers, onions, and the like. This was
lighted by three small windows, and furnished with a row of dressers filled with
crockery and kitchen ware, and permeated
by that savory smell which presages a generous breakfast   On one side of the fire-

place rested the great hominy mortar, cut from a tree trunk, found in all Virginia kitchens, and on the other the universal brick oven with its iron doors, — the very doors, I thought, that had closed over Chad's goose when Henny was a girl. Between the mortar and the oven opened, or rather caverned, a fireplace as wide as the colonel's hospitality, and high and deep enough to turn a coach in. It really covered one end of the room.

Bending over the swinging crane hung with pots and fringed with hooks, — baited so often with good dinners, — stood an old woman with bent back, her gray head bound up with a yellow handkerchief.

" Henny, de major made a special p'int o' comin' to see ye 'fo' he gits his breakfas'."

She looked up and dropped me a curt sey.

" Mawnin', marsa. I ain't much ter see, I 'm so ole an' mizzble wid dese yer cricks in my back an' sich a passel o' white folks. How did my Chad git along up dar 'mong de Yankees ? "

I gave Chad so good a character that every tooth in his head came out on dress

parade, and was about to draw from Henny
some of her own experiences, — this loyal
old servant whose life from her girlhood to
her old age had been one of the romantic
traditions of the roof that sheltered her, —
when Chad, who had gone out with the
roses, returned with the news that the colonel and his guests were breathing the morning air on the front porch, and were much
disturbed over my prolonged absence.

The colonel caught sight of me as I rounded the corner, Fitz and the agent joining in his outburst of hilarious welcome, intoxicated as they all were with the elixir of that most exhilarating of all hours — the hour before breakfast of a summer morning in the country.

"Welcome, my dear Major," called the colonel; "a hearty welcome to Caarter Hall! Come up here where you can get a view of Fairfax, suh!" and by the time I had mounted the steps he was leaning over the railing, with Fitz on the one side and the agent on the other, sweeping the horizon with his index finger and drawing imaginary curves and building bridges and locating railroad stations in the air with as much confidence and hope as if he really saw the gangs of laborers at work across the fields, their shovels glinting in the dazzling sunlight.

"Jes cast yo' eyes, suh," — this to the agent, — "and tell me, suh, if you have ever in yo' world-wide experience seen such a location for a great city. Level as a flo', watered by the Tench, and sheltered by a line of hills that are beauty itself — it is made for it, suh!"

The agent did full justice to the natural advantages and then asked : —

" Is the coal in that range ? "

" No, suh ; the coal is behind us on an outlyin' spur. I will take you there after breakfast."

And then followed a brief description of the changes the war had made in the homestead, the burning of the barns, the abandonment of the quarters, the destruction of the lawns — " A yard for their damnable wagons, suh ; " the colonel pointing out with great delight the very dent in the ridge where General Early had ridden through and captured the whole detachment without the loss of a man.

While we were talking that same rustling of silk that I had learned to know so well in Bedford Place was heard in the hall, then a sweet, cheery voice giving some directions to Chad, and the next instant dear aunt Nancy — Fitz and I had long since dared to call her so — floated (she never seemed to walk) out upon the porch with a word and a curtsey to the agent, a hand each to Fitz and me, and a kiss for the colonel.

Then came the breakfast, and such a

breakfast! The outpourings of a Virginia
kitchen, with the table showered with
roses, and the great urn shining and smoking, and the relays of waffles and corn-
bread and broiled chicken ; all in the old-
fashioned dining-room, with its high wain-
scoting, spindle - legged sideboards, and
deep window seats ; the long moon-faced
clock in the corner — and the rest of it!
After that the quiet smoke under the vine-
covered end of the portico with the view
towards Cartersville.

"There comes the jedge," said the colonel, pointing to a cloud of dust following
a two-wheel gig, "and Major Yancey behind on horseback." (They had both been
dropped outside their respective garden
gates the night before.) "Now, gentlemen, as soon as my attorney arrives with
the surveys and deeds we will adjourn to
my library and locate this coal-field."

Yancey's horse proved, on closer inspection, to be the remnant of an army mule
with a moth - eaten mane and a polished
tail bare of hair — worn off, no doubt, in a
lifelong struggle with the Fairfax County
fly. The major was without the luxury of
a saddle, some one having borrowed the

only one the owner of the mule possessed,
and his breeches, in consequence, were
half way up his knees. The judge arrived
in better shape, the gig being his own and
fairly comfortable, — the same he rode to

circuit, a yellow-painted vehicle washed
only when it rained, — and the horse the
property of the village livery man, who had
a yearly contract with his Honor for its
use.

Chad was waiting on the flagstones surrounded by some stray pickaninnies when
the procession stopped, and assisted the

major to alight, with as much form and
ceremony as if he had been the best
mounted gentleman in the land. The sad-
dleless fragment was then led to a supporting fence. The judicial equipage was ac-
corded the luxury of a shed, where the
annual contract was served with a full
measure of oats — Chad's recognition of
his more exalted station.

The judge bowed gracefully and with
great dignity, and with the air of a chief
justice entering the court room; then preceding the colonel and his guests, — without a word having fallen from his lips, —
he entered a small room opening into the
parlor. There he placed upon a chair
certain mysterious-looking packages, long
and otherwise, one a tin case, which he
uncapped, spreading its contents upon a
table.

It proved to be another and larger
map than the one Chad had pored over,
and showed distinctly the boundary lines
between two dots marked "Oak" and
"Rock" dividing the Carter and Barbour
estates.

Up to this time Fitz and the agent had
preserved the outward appearance of two

idle gentlemen visiting a friend in the country, with no interest beyond the fresh air and the environments of a charming hospitality. With the unrolling of this map, however, and the discovery of the very boundary points insisted on by Chad in Bedford Place, their excitement could hardly be suppressed. The agent broke loose first.

"Before we find out, Colonel Carter, to whom this coal belongs, which may take some valuable time, I want to examine the quality of the vein itself. I would like to go now."

"By all means, suh; and my people shall go with us," said the colonel, turning to Kerfoot with instructions to bring Chad and all the maps later. — Yancey excused himself on the ground of the heat. Then donning a wide straw hat and picking up a cane, — something he never used in New York, — the colonel led the way through the rear door, across a stone wall, and up a hill covered with a second growth of timber.

The experienced eye of the Englishman took in the lay of the land at a glance, and beckoning Fitz to one side he stooped

and picked something from the ground
which he examined carefully with a magni-
fying glass. Then they both disappeared
hurriedly over the hill.

When they returned, half an hour later,
the perspiration was rolling from the agent,
and Fitz's eyes were blazing. Both were
loaded down with bundles of broken bits
of rock, tied up in their several handker-
chiefs, large enough to start a geological
collection in a country museum.

"What is it, Fitz — diamonds?" I said,
laughing.

"Yes; black ones at that." He was almost breathless. "Solid bed of bitumin-
ous! Clear down to China! Don't breathe
a word yet, for your life!"

The agent was calmer. The coal-bed,
he said, seemed to be of more than ordinary richness, and as far as he could judge
lay in a vein of generous width. He was
ready for the survey, and would like the
boundary points located at once.

The next instant Chad's head peered
through the tangled underbrush. He carried the roll of maps, the judge, who followed, contenting himself with a package
tied with red tape.

The old darky's face was one broad grin from ear to ear.

The judge unrolled a map and placed it on a flat rock with a stone at each corner. Then he untied the package, selected an ink-stained and faded document marked "Deed — John Carter to E. A. Barbour," and ran his eye along the quaint page, reading as he went : —

Starting from an oak, blazed diamond C, ◇, along a line S. E. to a rock marked C cross B, C + B, in all a distance of 1437 linear feet.

"Now, Chad, we will fust find the tree," said the judge, looking around for his map-bearer. "Where's that nigger? Chad!"

The old man had disappeared as completely as if the earth had swallowed him up. The next minute we heard a faint halloo below us near the edge of a small swamp. A man was waving his hat and shouting : —

"Eve'ybody come yer!"

Fitz started on a run, and the agent and I followed on the double-quick. At the end of a crooked stone wall, half surrounded by water, was a great spreading oak, its branches reaching half way across the narrow marsh. Within touching distance of the yielding ground stood Chad pointing to a smooth blaze, stained and overgrown with lichen.

It bore this mark, ◈ !

"It tallies to a dot. Now, Chad, the rock! the rock!" said Fitz, hardly able to contain himself.

The darky pointed straight up the hill, the sky line of which could be seen entire from where we stood, and indicated an isolated rock jutting out above the tree-tops.

I thought Fitz would have hugged him.

"How do you know it is the rock with the crotch in it? Speak, you grinning lunatic!"

"I was dar dis mawnin' by daylight."

"What 's it marked?" said Fitz, catching him by both shoulders. "What 's it marked? Quick!"

"Wid a C an' a cross an' a •B — so." And the old man traced it with his finger in the mud.

"Every pound of coal on the colonel's land!" said Fitz, with a yell that brought his host and Kerfoot as fast as their legs could carry them.

"Stop!" said Kerfoot. "This only settles the Caarter and Barbour division.
There was another division here a year
ago between Miss Ann Caarter and the
colonel. With that I am mo' familiar, for
I drew the deeds, which are here," holding
up a bundle; "and I was also present with
the surveyor. You are wrong, Mr. Fitzpatrick; this entire hill outside the Barbour division is Miss Ann Caarter's, and
the coal is on her land. The colonel's portion is back there along the Tench."

CHAPTER XII

The Englishman's Check

An hour later I found Fitz flat on the grass under one of the apple-trees behind the house, completely broken up by the discoveries of the morning.

After all his work, here was the colonel worse off than ever. Nobody could tell what a woman would do. Aunt Nancy was better than the average (Fitz was a bachelor), but then she had peculiar old family notions about selling land, and ten chances to one she would not sell a foot of it, and there right in the house sat a man with his pocket full of blank checks, any one of which was good for a million of pounds sterling. Even if she did sell it, she would pension the dear old fellow off on a stipend instead of an establishment. He wanted somebody to dig a hole and cover Fitzpatrick up. Anybody could see that the railroad scheme was deader than a last year's pass, the farm hopeless, and

the house fast becoming a ruin. It was
enough to make a man jump off a dock.

Fitz's tirade was interrupted by Chad,
who appeared with a message. The colonel wanted everybody in the library.

When we entered, the judge occupied
the head of the table, surrounded by law
papers, all of which were opened. The
agent was bending over him, reading attentively, and entering extracts in his note-
book. Every one became seated.

"Mr. Fitzpatrick," said the agent, "I
have spent an hour with Judge Kerfoot
going over the title of this property, and I
am prepared to make a proposition for its
purchase. I have reduced it to writing,"
— picking up a half-sheet of foolscap from
the table, — "and I submit it to the owners
through you."

Fitz read it without changing a muscle,
and handed it to the colonel. Yancey and
the judge craned forward to catch the first
syllables.

The colonel read it to the end, getting
paler and paler as its meaning became
clear, and then, with a certain pathos in his
voice that was childlike, it was so genuine,
said : —

" If this is accepted, I presume, suh, you will not look any further into my road ? "

" You are right.   My instructions cover only the purchase of this deposit.   I have room for only one operation."

The colonel rose from his chair, steadied himself on the low window-sill, and looked out across the Tench.   The silence was oppressive — only the ticking of the clock in the next room and the bees among the flowers outside.

" Wait until I return," he said, crumpling the paper.

In a moment he was back, leading in his aunt by the hand.   Miss Nancy entered with a half-puzzled look on her face, which deepened into certain anxiety as she began to realize the pronounced formality of the proceedings.   The colonel cleared his throat impressively.

" Nancy, an investigation begun in New York by my dear friend Fitz, and completed here to-day, results in the discov'ry that what you have always considered as slight outcroppin's of coal, and wuthless, is really of vehy great value."   The colonel here unbuttoned his coat, and threw out his chest.   " A syndicate of English capital-

ists have, through our guest, offered you
the sum of one hundred thousand dollars
for the coal-hill, with a royalty of ten cents
per ton for every ton mined over a certain
amount, one thousand dollars to be paid
now and the balance on the search of title
and signin' of the contract. I believe I
have stated it correctly, suh ? "

The agent bowed his head, and scruti-
nized Miss Nancy's face with the eye of a
hawk.

The dear lady sank into a chair. For
a moment she lost her breath. Yancey
handed her a fan with a quickness of movement never seen in him before, and the
colonel continued : —

"This will of course still leave you,
Nancy, this house and about half of the
farm property transferred to you by me at
the fo'closure sale."

The little woman looked from one to the
other in a dazed sort of way, and her eye
rested on Fitz.

"What shall I do, Mr. Fitzpatrick? It
seems to me a grave step to sell any part
of the estate."

Fitz blushed at the mark of her confidence, and said that with the royalty

clause he thought the proposition a favorable one.

"And you, George?" turning to the colonel.

The colonel bowed his head. He must advise its acceptance.

"When do you want an answer, sir?"

"To-day, Madam," said the Englishman, who had not taken his eyes from her face.

"You shall have it in half an hour," she said gently, then rose hastily, and left the room.

I looked at the colonel. Whatever great wave of disappointment had swept over him when his own idol was broken, there was no trace of it in his face. Even the change this sudden influx of wealth into the family might make in his own condition never seemed to have crossed his mind. He did not follow her. He simply waited. Between his own plans and his aunt's good fortune there was but one course for him.

The room took on the whispered silence of a court awaiting an overdue jury. Fitz was still incredulous and still anxious, saying to me in an undertone that he felt sure she would either refuse it altogether or couple it with some conditions that the agent could not accept; either would be fatal. Yancey and the judge, who had been partly paralyzed at the rapidity of the transaction, conferred in a corner, while the agent proceeded to make a copy of the proposition with as much composure as if he bought a coal-mine every day. The colonel sat by himself, his chair tilted back, his eyes half closed.

In the midst of this uncertainty Chad entered with a message. "Miss Nancy wants de colonel." In five minutes more he entered with another. Miss Nancy wanted Fitz and me.

We followed the old servant up the winding staircase and down the long hall, past the old-fashioned wardrobe and the great chintz-covered lounge, waited until Chad knocked gently, and entered the dear lady's bedroom.

She sat near the window by the side of the high post bedstead, rocking gently to and fro. The colonel was standing with his back to the light, coat open, thumbs in his armholes, face beaming.

"I sent for you," she began, "because I want you both to hear my answer before I inform the agent. The land only was

mine, and but for your love and devotion
to the colonel would still be a wild hill.
The coal, therefore, belongs to him.   Go
and tell the Englishman I accept his
offer.   The land and all the coal I give to
George."

When, an hour later, the transaction was
complete, the receipts and preliminary con-
tracts signed, and the small, modest-looking
check — the first instalment — had been
transferred from the plethoric bank-book
of the agent to the narrow, poverty-stricken
pocket of the colonel, and the fact began
to dawn simultaneously upon everybody
that at last the dear old colonel was inde-
pendent, an enthusiasm took possession of
the room that soon became uncontrollable.

Fitz caught him in his arms, and began
hugging him in a way that endangered
every rib in his body, calling out all the time
that he had never felt so good in all the days
of his life.   Yancey and Kerfoot, who had
stood one side appalled by the magnitude
of the sum paid, and who during the sign-
ing of the papers had looked at the colonel
with the same sort of silent awe with which
they would have regarded any other po-

tentate rolling in estates, mines, and millions, broke through the enforced reserve,
and exclaimed, with an outburst, that the
South was looking up, and that a true
Southern gentleman had come into his
own, the judge adding with emphasis that
the colonel had never looked so much like
his noble father as when he stooped over
and signed that receipt.   Even the Englishman, hard, practical fellow that he was,
congratulated him on his good fortune in a
few short words that jumped out hot from
his heart.

With this atmosphere about him it is not
to be wondered that the colonel lost the
true inwardness of the situation.   The fact
that his aunt's boundary line included every
acre of valuable land on the plantation,
while his own poor portion only bordered
the Tench, was to him simply one of those
trifling errors which sometimes occur in
the partition of vast landed estates.   And
although when the gift was made he felt
more than ever her loving-kindness, he
could not now, on more mature reflection
and after hearing the encomiums of his
friends, really see how she could have pur-
sued any other course.

And yet, with the sale accomplished and
he rich beyond his wildest dreams, he was
precisely the same man in bearing, manner,
and speech that he had been in his impe-
cunious days in Bedford Place.   He was
rich then — in hopes, in plans, in the reality
of his dreamland.   He was no richer now.
The check in his pocket made no difference.

The only perceptible change was when
he recounted to me his plans for the res-
toration of the homestead and the comfort of its inmates.   "I shall rebuild the
barns and cabins, and lay out a new lawn.
The po'ch" — looking up — "needs some
repairs, and the ca'iage-house must be en-
larged.   The coaching days are not over
yet, Major; Nancy must have" —

Chad, entering with a luncheon for the
exhausted circle, diverted the colonel's train
of thought, cutting short his summary.   For
a moment he watched his old servant mus-
ingly, then following him into the next room
he called him to one side, and with marked
tenderness in his manner unfolded the Englishman's check.

The old servant put down the empty
tray, adjusted his spectacles, and examined
it carefully.

"What's dis, Marsa George?"

"A thousand dollars, Chad."

"Golly! Monst'ous quare kind o' money. Jes a scrap. Ain't big enough to wad a gun, is she? An' Misser Englishman gib ye dis for dat ole brier patch?"

Chad was trembling all over, full to the very eyelids.

The colonel held out his hand. The old servant bent his head, his master's hand fast in his. Then their eyes met.

"Yes, Chad, for you and me. There's no hard work for you any mo', old man. Go and tell Henny."

That night at dinner, Fitz on the colonel's right, the Englishman next to aunt Nancy, Kerfoot, Yancey, and I disposed in regular order, Chad noiseless and attentive, the colonel arose in his chair, radiant to the very tip ends of his cravat, and, in a voice which trembled as it rose, said : —

"Gentlemen, the events of the day have unexpectedly brought me an influx of wealth far beyond my brightest anticipations. This is due in great measure to the untirin' brain and vast commercial resources of my dear friend Mr. Fitzpatrick, who has labored with me durin' my sojourn Nawth in the development of these properties, and who now, with that unselfishness which caaracterizes his life, refuses to accept any share in the result.

" They have also strengthened the tie existin' between my old friend the major on my left, who oftentimes when the day was darkest has cheered me by his counsel and companionship.

" But, gentlemen, they have done mo'." The colonel's feet now barely touched the floor.   " They have enabled me to provide for one of the loveliest of her sex, — she who graces our boa'd, — and to enrich her declinin' days not only with all the comforts, but with many of the luxuries she was bawn to enjoy.

" Fill yo' glasses, gentlemen, and drink to the health of that greatest of all bless= ings, — a true Southern lady ! "

Printed in the United States
41661LVS00014B/66